Starshine!

ELLEN SCHWARTZ

POLESTAR
BOOK PUBLISHERS

Fourth printing, 1994

Published by Polestar Press Ltd.
1011 Commercial Drive, Second Floor
Vancouver, BC
Canada   V5L 3X1

The publisher would like to thank the Canada Council, the British Columbia Ministry of Small Business, Tourism and Culture, and the Department of Canadian Heritage for their ongoing financial assistance.

Special thanks to Sue Ann Alderson for her help with the manuscript, and to Reesa Smith for her arachnological information.

Cover illustration and design by Jim Brennan
Interior illustrations by Laura Wallace
Printed in Canada by Hignell Printers Ltd.

Canadian Cataloguing in Publication Data

Schwartz, Ellen, 1949-
      Starshine!

ISBN 0-919591-24-8
      I. Title-.
PS8587.C53S8   1987   jC813'.54   C87-091488-X
PZ7.S25St 1987

for Merri and Amy

Chapter One

I HATE MY name. My mom says all kids hate their names, but I really do. It's horrendous. Anything would be better than my name. I'd take Gertrude, Myrtle, even Wilhemina. But no, I had to get stuck with — Are you ready? Hold your nose — STARSHINE BLISS SHAPIRO.

Is that the most obnoxious name in the world, or what? I was born at about three o'clock in the morning, and my mom looked out the window and saw a star and named me Starshine. And then my parents were so happy to have me, they stuck on Bliss for a middle name.

Can you imagine the razzing I get at school? "Quick, put on your sunglasses, here comes Starshine!" Jimmy Tyler always says. Miranda Stockton's favorite is "Twinkle, twinkle, little Starshine." Ha, ha, very funny.

At home everyone calls me Star — well, my little sister Peggy says "Stah," but she can't pronounce r's yet. I wish it had been a cloudy night when I was born and my mom didn't see that star. But then she probably would have named me Cloud-cover or something. When you're eighteen you can change your name. I'm going to change mine to Ann Jane Shapiro. I only have nine years to go.

When my parents had me, they were living in a little cabin in the woods, growing vegetables and raising goats and honeybees and gathering wild flowers for tea. My mom says people who lived like that were called hippies and they were trying to do their own thing and change the world. I don't see how living in the woods changes the world, but I do know that even though we moved to

Vancouver, my mom and dad are still doing their own thing. They don't have regular jobs like most people. My mom is a potter and my dad is a stained glass artist. They work in a big workshop next to Peggy's room. And Peggy says — well, let me tell you about her.

She's chubby and has a button nose and rosy cheeks. She's two and a half. She has temper tantrums over the stupidest things. Like, if you tell her to pick up her teddy bear, she flops onto the floor, kicking her feet and screaming. Of course, she stops every couple minutes to make sure you're watching. Then she turns off the tears, picks up the teddy bear, and is all smiley again. What an actress!

Still, Peggy and I get along pretty good. We have great tickle fights. But there's one thing I'll never forgive her for: her name. "Peggy" is so nice and plain. So normal. I asked my dad why they didn't name *her* something weird. He said, "Well, Star, I guess we mellowed out." I don't know what mellowed out means. Maybe chickened out. All I know is, I got the raw deal in the name department.

My dad's name is Peter. He's chubby around the middle and has the deepest belly button I've ever seen. (I haven't seen that many belly buttons, but I'd put his up against anybody's.) He's mostly bald, with some brown hair around the edges. His beard tickles when we hug. My dad doesn't talk a lot. Instead he whistles all the time. I can always tell where he is by his whistling. He's calm. When everyone gets into a flap, he gets us out of it.

My mom is super-energetic. My dad calls her the Energy Queen, but actually her name is Joan. She's skinny. She has big brown eyes, a hooked nose ("my beak," she calls it), and black wavy hair. Everyone says I look just like her. I'm glad, because I think she's real pretty — but I hope I don't get a beak when I grow up.

My mom's really into her pottery. I think it's neat that she loves what she does. But sometimes she gets carried away. When she's working on a pot she's in another world. If you talk to her, she either doesn't hear you or practically bites your head off. Then, when she finally gets the pot the way she likes it — she says she's "giving birth" to it — she's happy again. I've learned to wait until she's given birth to ask for a special favor or tell bad news, like I've ripped the knees out of my new tights, which I wasn't supposed to be wearing while I was riding my bike in the first place.

Everybody thinks that just because my mom and dad are artistic, I should be, too. I'm not. I mean, I can draw OK, but nothing special. I can just about carry a tune. Forget dancing. I took ballet once, and the teacher told my mom, "I believe her talents lie elsewhere." You know what that means: "Your kid's a klutz, lady."

I do like making up stories, though — and with a two-and-a-half-year-old sister, I get lots of practice. Sometimes I act out my stories for Peggy. But never for anyone else. I'd be too embarrassed to do that.

No, I'm not the creative type. I'm just a normal kid.... Well, there is one unusual thing about me. I love spiders. I'm going to be an arachnologist when I grow up. That's a person who studies arthropods, such as spiders and scorpions.

You should see my room. Well, maybe you shouldn't. I've got five copies of *Charlotte's Web* — two hardcover and three paperback. One whole bookshelf is full of books on spiders. For my last birthday I got the *Field Guide to Spiders of the Americas*. It's 287 pages long and weighs about a ton. I've also got pictures of spiders on the walls. One is of a burrowing wolf spider sitting in its burrow. I call her Josephine. Another is of a lynx spider with little prickly

things on his legs and a mean gleam in his eye. That's Herman.

Sometimes I mount spiders on my bulletin board. Dead, of course. I don't believe in catching live animals. I stick them on with a pin. The only trouble is that once they're dead, their bodies dry out. After a few days, when you touch them, POOF! They crumble into dust. There's an awful pile of dust under my bulletin board.

My parents aren't too crazy about spiders. My mom says, "Birds I could see. Fish, even. But spiders?" And my dad, I think, is scared of them, though he doesn't admit it. I figure if they knew interesting things, like the fact that most spiders have eight eyes, they'd like them. But they always change the subject. Silly, aren't they?

Just like the kids in my class. Last year, in grade three, I brought a nursery web spider into school for Show and Tell. It was dead but in great shape. I held it in the palm of my hand and told the class about nursery webs. Nobody seemed terribly interested but at least no one freaked out. (That was an improvement over grade two.)

But then Miranda Stockton blew it. She's got blond hair that she wears with a barrette that says MIRANDA, and she's always got hot pink fingernail polish on and shiny black shoes that she never, ever, gets dirty. Her desk was right in front of mine. During spelling, one of her hair ribbons came untied and slipped down the back of her shirt. She thought I'd put my spider on her — as if I'd let it touch *her* — and started wiggling around and screaming, "Help! Get it off me! It's crawling down my back!" Everyone laughed and she realized it wasn't the spider. Her face turned all red. I could tell she felt really stupid and I even felt sorry for her.

But then she started taking it out on me. She giggled and

said, "What's it like living in a cobweb, Starshine?" Some kids laughed. "Hey, now that I look at you, you do kind of look like your little pet there," she added. There was more laughter and a few kids joined the teasing. I felt rotten. I mean, I hadn't done anything — except like spiders. But Miranda's popular and kids like to tease and that's how it goes. Anyway, after that I never took spiders into school. It was just one more way that I was different from the other kids. And there are enough of those.

Like the fact that I'm a vegetarian. Instead of meat, my family eats stuff like brown rice and cheese casserole, spaghetti and nut balls made with ground nuts, and lentil loaf. I guess these dishes sound awful if you're not a vegetarian, but they're really delicious. But I bet I'm the only kid in grade four — no, probably the whole school — who has never eaten a hamburger or a hot dog. Don't tell anyone that. The only person who knows is Julie, my best friend. I can trust her. After all, it was food that brought us together.

It was the first week of school this year and the day I had been dreading: Hot Dog Day. That's when the school sells hot dogs for lunch. I always hate Hot Dog Day because I'm the only one with a different kind of lunch. Everybody goes bonkers over hot dogs. If you don't eat them they think you're un-Canadian or an animal hater or something.

I think *they're* nuts. I mean, doesn't it make sense that if you don't eat hot dogs, you're doing pigs a favor? Think of poor Wilbur in *Charlotte's Web*. Can you imagine eating him? Besides, I've heard that pigs are quite smart and can be trained to do tricks and stuff, and I'd hate to think of eating one. But that's not how the other kids feel. If you're not crazy about hot dogs, you're out of it.

On this day, Ms. Rooney, our teacher, had just told the

class to line up to go to the gym to buy their hot dogs. All the kids — except me — were standing in line, laughing and pushing, jingling their coins and bragging about how many hot dogs they were going to eat with mustard, relish, and "the works," whatever that means. I felt totally left out. But I wasn't going to show it. Putting my best "I-don't-care" look on my face, I got my lunch box and went back to my desk. Very carefully, so no one could see, I opened the lid.

I closed it right away. I couldn't believe it. On the first Hot Dog Day at Priscilla Marpole Elementary School, my mother had given me a tofu burger for lunch.

Now, tofu burgers are my favorite dish in the whole world. So when I opened my lunch box, I thought, Yummers! My mom had put it in a homemade whole wheat bun with some alfalfa sprouts and a little mayonnaise on the bun, just the way I like it. But a tofu burger on Hot Dog Day? I pictured Jimmy Tyler and Tommy Scott coming over to me with their hands full of hot dogs, dripping mustard all over the place. Jimmy would say, "What *is* that stuff?" And Tommy would say, "I don't know, I think it's dog food!" And Jimmy would say, "Don't get too close, it might be catching!"

I tried to figure out what to do. Could I eat the whole thing before the kids came back into the classroom? No, it was too big. I'd choke if I tried. Could I say, "Oh, it's a mnpfm burger," and hope nobody asked me to explain? No, I probably couldn't get away with it. Could I explain that tofu is made from soybeans and is really good for you? No, they wouldn't care.

So I decided not to eat lunch. I knew that was stupid. I knew it was a great big cop-out. But it was the only thing I could think of. I just didn't feel like being teased.

I sat there drumming my fingers on my lunch box. My stomach growled. I tried not to think about food. I thought about the spelling test we'd just had. I'd aced it. I'm a good speller. I thought about the spelling words. Arrogance. Preparation. Banquet. I thought about a banquet table full of food. My stomach growled again. I thought about the tofu burger and the whole wheat bun and the alfalfa sprouts. I put my finger on the clasp of my lunch box.

Just then I turned around to make sure no one was watching me, and I saw her. A girl was sitting in the last seat in the row near the windows. She was a new kid. I tried to think of her name. Jenny? Judy? Then I remembered: Julie. Julie Wong. She seemed like a nice kid but kind of shy. Even though she was Chinese, she had an English accent. That made me curious but I didn't know her well enough yet to ask her about it. Now there she was in the last seat, holding a little bowl under her mouth and eating something with chop sticks.

I turned back around and rested my chin on my hands. My stomach growled again. Be quiet, I told it. Don't remind me. Then a wonderful thought came into my head: Julie wasn't eating a hot dog. She had brought her lunch from home, too. I wasn't the only one!

I picked up my lunch box, practically skipped down the aisle to the desk across from hers, and sat down. Grinning, I said, "You don't eat hot dogs?"

"No." She pointed at her food with her chop sticks. "My mother says this is more nutritious." She pronounced mother "muth-ah," very British. And she smiled, as if to say, You know how mothers are.

"Well, I don't either," I said, and opened my lunch box. I took out the tofu burger and took a big bite. Mmmm... delish.

Julie turned sideways in her seat facing me. When she leaned forward to take a bite, her black hair swung forward in a smooth wave and then swung back again. I liked the way it shimmered. And boy, was she good with those chop sticks. I'll have to get her to show me how, I thought.

"What are you eating?" Julie said.

I held the half-eaten tofu burger out to show her. "A tofu burger. You've probably never heard of tofu — "

"Oh no?" She smiled, then held out her bowl and poked around with a chop stick. "What do you think this is?"

I looked. Sure enough, in among the rice and bits of meat and vegetables were little white squares of tofu. I grinned at her and she grinned back. We both started giggling as the first kids came back into the room with their hot dogs.

Chapter Two

AFTER THAT Julie and I got to be best friends. She told me she was from Hong Kong. Before she came to Canada, she went to a private school and learned English from an Englishman, and that was why she had an English accent.

Most days after school we went to Riley Park to play. One day when we were hanging upside down from the monkey bars, she told me she wanted to be an actress when she grew up. I said, "Great," only it came out more like "Grnpt." I pulled myself up and said, "You'll be terrific."

"Oh, Stah Dah-link, do you rolly think so?" Julie said, sitting up.

I started laughing and almost let go of the bar. I did think so, though. She was always switching accents and getting dramatic. Like, if I said, "I can't come to the park today," she'd start pretend-crying and say, "Oh, no, don't say that, how can you be so crue-ell?" and fall to the floor in a heap.

Julie turned sideways on the bar to face me. "Star, do you think I should change my name? When I'm an actress, I mean."

"No, why?"

"Well, 'Julie Wong' is kind of dull."

"Don't complain," I said.

"But it's not dramatic," she argued.

"You want a dramatic name?"

She nodded.

"Trade you," I said quickly.

Julie grinned. "Uh... no thanks."

I grinned back. "Didn't think so," I said.

All of a sudden it began to rain. First there were only a few drops. Then it started coming down harder. We couldn't stay outside. I secretly hoped Julie would invite me to her house. For one thing I was curious about her family — besides her and her parents there were two older brothers, one younger brother and her grandparents. For another, I thought she'd probably hate my weird family. But she said her brothers always made such a racket, we'd be better off at my place. I wasn't so sure about that, but I said OK. Holding our math books over our heads, we ran to my house.

When we came inside, there was a pile of about five pairs of Peggy's shoes on the doormat. You see, Peggy has a thing about shoes. She hates to wear them. She goes around the house leaving a trail of sneakers, sandals, and Oscar the Grouch slippers behind her.

I'm used to it, of course, so I stepped right over the pile. But Julie walked into it. Then she looked down and saw the shoes. I pushed them aside with my foot. "My little sister doesn't believe in wearing shoes," I explained, trying to make it sound like a joke.

"Oh," Julie said. But she wasn't looking at the shoes anymore. She was looking at the windows. Most houses have regular windows. We've got stained glass ones. On sunny days the sun shines through and throws red, green, yellow, purple and blue patches on the floor and walls. It's pretty. But on gloomy days the house looks like a dark, lonely church. This was a gloomy day.

Julie didn't seem to mind, though. "I like your windows," she said.

"My dad made them."

"Yeah?" She looked from one window to another. "Neat."

I heard the hum of the potter's wheel from the workshop and my dad's whistling from somewhere outside. Suddenly there was a yell, "Stah!" Peggy came charging across the living room, flung herself at me, wrapped her arms around my legs, and looked up at me, beaming. She had nothing on from the waist down, her hands were covered with green playdough, and her mouth and chin were coated with peanut butter.

"This is Peggy," I said to Julie. "Peg, this is Julie."

Julie looked down at Peggy's filthy face. "Hi, Peggy," she said.

Peggy didn't answer. She started kissing my leg, smearing peanut butter all over my pants. "She likes peanut butter," I said to Julie.

"But not shoes," Julie said.

"Right." Trying to push Peggy away, I said, "Enough kisses, Peg." She switched to the other leg.

Julie pretended not to notice the mess my pants were getting into. "Doesn't she get cold... like that?"

"Well, she's getting toilet trained," I said. Julie had a younger brother. I hoped she understood.

At the words "toilet trained," Peggy let go of me and turned to Julie. "I go pee an' poo in poh-tee," she said importantly.

"Oh... that's nice," Julie said.

With a grin, Peggy turned back to me. She sucked a big gob of peanut butter off my pant leg, and then toddled away.

"Let's go say hi to my mom," I said before Julie could say anything about my obnoxious sister. As we walked through the living room Julie said, "You've sure got a lot of cups in your house."

"Only about three zillion," I said.

Julie laughed. But I wasn't kidding. Our house is overflowing with cups — cups with twisty handles, cups shaped like birds, cups with faces carved on the sides. My mom was really into cups for a while. Now it's bowls.

"My mom's working on a bowl in the shape of a dragon," I told Julie.

"A dragon," Julie repeated, nodding her head as if everybody's mom made bowls in the shape of dragons.

I opened the workshop door and Julie followed me in. Peggy was at the little table in the corner. Part of the workshop is a play area so my mom and dad can keep an eye on her. She was mushing green playdough. My mom was at the potter's wheel. Her hair waved out wildly around her head. Her face, arms, and the whole front of her apron were flecked with dabs of orangey-brown clay. She was talking to the dragon bowl.

"Hi, Mom," I said.

"Not now," she said without looking up.

It was one of those days. I motioned to Julie to follow me and we left the workshop.

"She's always like that when she's about to give birth," I said.

"Oh, really? She didn't look — "

"No, no," I interrupted, realizing what she thought, "not that kind of birth. Giving birth to the pot."

"To the pot?"

"It's — uh, an expression in pottery," I fibbed, then pretended not to see the funny look Julie gave me. "Let's go up to my room," I said. As we walked back through the living room, I heard my dad's whistling again from outside the house. I couldn't imagine what he was doing out there in the rain.

We started up the stairs. Our house has a winding stair-case that doesn't just make one or two turns, it makes four. Just as Julie and I reached the first landing, there was a loud scratching noise on our right, and then a saw poked through the wall above us. Sawdust fell on our heads. With a gasp, Julie jumped into my arms. The saw screeched backward and disappeared. A second later it came through again, spraying us with more sawdust.

I knew what was happening. My dad was cutting a hole in the wall to put one of his stained glass windows in.

The saw started going out again. Julie jerked. I thought she was going to have a heart attack right in my arms. "DAD!" I yelled as loud as I could. The saw stopped halfway out. I heard my dad climb down the ladder, and a few seconds later his face appeared at the living room window. "Hi, Star."

"Dad, could you do that another time?"

He looked puzzled. "Why?"

"Well, I have a friend over and — "

"You're not playing on the stairs, are you?"

"No, but — well, you scared her with the saw."

Rainwater dripped from the hood of his raincoat onto the tip of his nose. "Star, I've got the ladder and saw out here, I'm halfway done — "

"Dad, *please*."

He opened his mouth to speak, shut it, opened it again and said, "OK." He left. A moment later the saw disappeared back through the hole.

Julie untangled herself from my arms. She shook her head and sawdust flew in every direction. Glancing fear-fully at the hole, she moved toward the banister, away from the wall. We continued climbing. "Sorry about that," I began. "You see, my dad's an artist, and — well, my mom, too, and she's kind of — I mean, my sister — oh, never mind." It was no use trying to explain. I pictured Julie at the dinner table that night, telling her family about her visit to my house. "... and then this saw came through the wall...." Her parents would probably never let her come over again.

We went up to my room. I started taking off my peanut buttery, playdoughy pants. Julie stopped in the doorway and stared at the spider posters. I thought it might be a good idea to make introductions. "Julie, meet Josephine and Herman," I said, putting on a pair of jeans and a sweatshirt.

"How do you do?" she said with a little shudder. Then she saw the bulletin board. There was a circle of little garden spiders with a big nursery web spider in the middle.

"Uh, Star?" she said.

"Yeah?"

"Those aren't alive, are they?"

"Of course not," I said. "Do you think I'd put pins through live spiders?"

"How would I know?"

"Well, just imagine you were a spider," I said, "and someone stuck a big pin through you. I bet you'd — "

"Starshine!" she interrupted. "I believe you. Honest." She leaned a little closer. "Boy, they sure have a lot of eyes, don't they?"

"Eight," I said. "Most of the arachnids have — "

"The arach — what?"

"Arachnids," I said. "That's what spiders are. It's their scientific name. They're named after Arachne."

"Who's he?" Julie sat down on the bed.

"Not he, she."

"Oh. What's her name again?"

"Arachne." I went over to my chalkboard and picked up a piece of chalk. Pretending I was a teacher, I said, "Now, class, this is how you spell Arachne." I printed it in capital letters, then said, "You will have a test on this tomorrow."

"Right," she said with a smirk. "That looks like it would be pronounced A-*ratch*-nee."

"I know," I agreed. "But it's pronounced A-*rack*-nee."

"Oh. Well, anyway, who is she?"

I sat down next to Julie. "She's Greek. I mean, she *was* Greek. She lived a long time ago. She's in myths."

"Did she like spiders too?" Julie asked.

I shook my head. "Arachne was a peasant girl. She was a terrific weaver. She said that her weaving was the best in the world. That made Athena mad."

"Athena?"

"Yeah. One of the goddesses. She was a real good weaver, too. She couldn't stand the idea of a girl being a better weaver than her, since she was a goddess and all. So they had a contest."

"Who won?"

"Well, they both did their best weaving," I went on. "Athena's was beautiful, but Arachne's was even better. Athena got mad. She ripped up Arachne's weaving and started beating her with her shuttle. Then Arachne was so embarrassed, she hung herself."

"Oh-h-h," Julie said sadly.

"Wait. That's not the end. Athena felt kind of sorry, so she brought Arachne back to life and changed her into a spider so she could go on weaving forever and ever."

Julie was quiet for a minute. Then she said, "Nice story. Kind of sad and happy at once."

I nodded. "That's why spiders are called arachnids.

Scorpions are arachnids, too, only they — "

"Star," Julie interrupted, holding up her hand. "I hate to hurt your feelings, but I really don't feel like hearing about scorpions right at this moment."

"OK, I get the hint," I said. "How about a snack?"

We went downstairs. I got some of my dad's health food cookies out of the cookie jar and put them on a plate. Julie picked one up and took a bite. Her teeth didn't even sink in. She took it out of her mouth and looked at it. Uh-oh, I thought, I forgot to tell Julie about bricks.

My dad invented bricks. When Peggy was a baby, he was making some teething cookies for her one day. He threw together a whole bunch of healthy stuff like soy flour and blackstrap molasses, put the dough in the oven, and forgot all about it. By the time he remembered, the cookies were baked as hard as bricks.

My dad gave one to Peggy. She loved it. She drooled and slobbered over it and mushed it up with her gums and kept out of everybody's hair for a whole hour. My dad said that any cookie that could do that was a huge success.

At first I refused to eat them. But one day after school I was really starved and there was nothing else in the house. I took a brick, dunked it in my milk to soften it up and, you know, it really wasn't too bad. Kind of like a molasses-flavored dog biscuit. So now I eat them all the time.

Julie held the brick between two fingers and looked at me. "Uh... Star?"

For a second I thought of telling her it was a new kind of building toy, like Lego or something. The latest. All the kids have them. You can build 64 different kinds of houses with them.

But then why would they be on a plate? And why would

I have served them with milk? "They're cookies," I said.

Before Julie could answer, I smelled something. Something stinky. A moment later there was the patter of little bare feet and in came Peggy carrying her white potty. "Look, Stah! Look, Doo-ee!"

I stood between Peggy and Julie. "Peggy! Gross!"

She wiggled around me and held the container out to Julie. "I made poo in poh-tee. See?"

Julie took a deep breath and held it. "Love-ly, Peg-gy," she said, letting out little bursts of air.

"Aw by my-seff," Peggy added.

Julie nodded. Her face started turning red. If she didn't breathe soon, she was going to pass out.

I took Peggy by the shoulders and turned her around. "We don't care. Go show Mom." She marched out of the kitchen, leaving a smelly trail behind her.

Julie let out the breath in a noisy sigh. She took several deep breaths, then said, "I'm not hungry anymore."

"Me neither," I said. "Let's go out on the back porch."

Chapter Three

W E STEPPED outside. It was drizzling now. We sat on the swing chair that my dad built and rocked slowly back and forth. Creak-groan, creak-groan, creak-groan, went the swing chair.

I was so embarrassed I couldn't even look at Julie. Why did Peggy have to do that on the very first day she came over, I thought. And Dad with his saw. And Mom with her bad mood. Now Julie probably thinks *I'm* weird. Maybe she'll never come over again.

We rocked without talking. Creak-groan, creak-groan. I picked up a Nerf ball that was lying on the swing chair. "Throw," Julie said. I looked at her. She was smiling. I tossed it to her. She threw it back. I threw it back, harder. She batted it back at me. We started giggling. I slammed it at her, shouting, "Take that!" The ball bounced off her head and rolled into the corner.

"Foul!" she yelled, and ran to get the ball. "Yuck, it's full of yellow cobwebs." She came back holding the ball with two fingers.

"Yellow cobwebs?" I said, jumping off the swing chair. I ran to the corner and looked closely. "Wow!"

Julie jumped and dropped the ball. She came over and stood behind me. "What is it?"

"Julie, I can't believe it! Holy cow! Wait a minute, I'll be right back." I raced up to my room and came back out with the *Field Guide to Spiders of the Americas*. Breathing hard, I flipped through the pages until I found the one I wanted. I peered into the corner, back at the book, into the corner again. Then I turned around and hugged Julie, banging her with the field guide. "Julie, you're wonderful! Oh, sorry. Wow!"

She pushed me away. "Hey, let go! Why am I wonderful!"

"'Cause you found it," I said, and crouched down again to look.

"WHAT?" she shouted.

"The golden silk spider," I told her. "*Nephilia*. See?" I pointed to a picture in the book.

"So?"

"SO?" I yelled. "Julie — The golden silk! It's — it's — incredible! They only live in warm places. I don't know how this one got to Vancouver. It's amazing! And you found it."

"No, I didn't. All I did was say 'Yuck.'"

I bent down to have another look. The spider was spinning like crazy, trying to fix its golden-yellow web.

"I think I'd better go home now," Julie said.

"Don't you want to have a look under the magnifying glass?" I said.

"No, thanks."

"Oh, come on."

"No, really, it's OK," Julie said, backing away.

I walked her to the front door. Even though I was excited about the spider, I couldn't let her go without making sure we were still friends. "Uh... Julie," I said, kicking at Peggy's shoes with my toe, "about my family — I mean, I hope you don't think — " I swallowed. "I'm sorry if you didn't have a good time."

She looked at me like I was crazy. "What are you talking about? I had a great time."

"Yeah?"

"Yeah," she said with a smile, and left.

I ran upstairs, got my new magnifying glass, and carried it downstairs very, very carefully. I'd just bought it with my own allowance. It cost $11.95 plus tax. Do you know how long it took me to save up that much? Forever, that's how long. My piggy bank is empty.

The spider was beautiful. It was easy to tell it was a girl because it was so big. Boy golden webs are tiny. Her body was greenish brown with white spots. There were bunches of hair on her legs. Under the magnifying glass, the hairs looked as smooth as cat's fur.

But what's a tropical spider doing in Canada? I wondered. Then I felt some warm air on my back. I turned around. There was a plant hanging from a hook in the ceiling, the kind with long trailing vines and big leaves. I pushed the leaves aside. A pipe stuck out of the wall. The warm air was coming from it. I remembered that my mom and dad's workshop was on the other side of the wall. This pipe must carry heat away from my mom's kiln. And maybe the warm air was keeping the spider alive. But that didn't explain how she got there in the first place.

I watched her weave. Sometimes she stopped and hung perfectly still. Then she scurried from one side of the web to the other, trailing a golden thread.

The next thing I knew, my mom was calling me in for supper. I sat down at the table. My mom handed me a plate and said, "Papaya, Star?"

"Yum," I said, taking a piece. "Hey, Mom, do you have lots of pots to make?"

"Yes. Why?"

"'Cause there's a golden silk spider on the porch, and I think it needs the hot air from the kiln."

"I made poo in poh-tee," Peggy announced. Since she's just getting toilet trained, we're supposed to encourage her to use the potty instead of her diaper or the floor. So we all said, "Good girl, Peggy."

My mom turned to me. "I don't get it. What does my kiln have to do with this spider?"

"'Cause it's a golden silk," I said. "*Nephilia*. See?" I showed her the picture in the field guide, which was next to my plate.

"Big poo," Peggy said.

"That's nice, Peggy," my dad said. My mom reached over and patted her on the head, then motioned me to close the book. "No books at the table, Star. Now, what about this golden thread — "

"Silk," I said. "Golden silk. They only live in warm — "

"Big, big poo," said Peggy.

"Peggy!" I yelled.

"Don't shout, Star," my dad said. He turned to Peggy. "You're interrupting, Pumpkin. Be quiet and wait your turn, OK?"

Peggy nodded her head very seriously. Sure, I thought, she'll be quiet for at least ten seconds.

My mom took a slice of papaya and started eating it. "Mmmm," she said, "the taste of the tropics."

"That's what I'm trying to tell you," I said. "The golden silk spider lives in the tropics. I don't know how this one got onto our porch, but it did. And the warm air from your kiln — "

"I a good girl," said Peggy.

My parents ignored her, for once. They looked at each other with a sick look on their faces. Both turned slightly yellow. My dad lifted up his plate and looked underneath. My mom went to the garbage can and took out a plastic bag. You could see the bag was empty, but she shook it anyway. Nothing came out.

At first I didn't understand. Then I got it. Papayas grow in tropical countries. The spider must have hitched a ride with the papayas. Somehow she got into the bag my mom bought. And then she escaped and made it to the back porch.

"Neat-o!" I said. "Just think — maybe she wasn't even hatched yet when you bought the papayas! She was still in the egg sac!"

"Egg sac?" said my dad, turning yellower.

"Is it poisonous?" my mom asked.

Shaking my head, I patted the field guide. "No, I checked."

"Thank goodness for that," my dad said. Then he added, "Star, could you... uh, move it somewhere else? Off the porch?"

"How about a nice cozy spot along the back fence?" my mom suggested.

"No," I said. "She's used to warm weather. I'm pretty sure she needs the warm air from the kiln." My dad opened his mouth, but before he could speak, I added, "It's really amazing to find a golden silk this far north."

They looked at each other. Then my mom said, "All right, Star. It — she — whatever it is — can stay on the porch. But it better not come into the house. Ever. OK?"

"OK," I answered. That was fine with me. I just hoped the spider would make it out there. I decided to be extra good and pick up after myself so my mom would have more time to make pots and keep the kiln going.

As soon as supper was over I went upstairs and wrote a letter to the American Association of Arachnology. I told them the whole story, how the Nerf ball rolled into the corner and Julie said "Yuck" and I found the spider. I told them exactly what it looked like and how the web looked. And how my mom bought some papayas at the fruit store, and maybe that was where the spider came from. And how that corner of the porch is outside of my mom and dad's workshop and about the pipe, and did they think that's why the *Nephilia* picked that spot, and would the warm air keep her alive?

The letter took up two whole pages. By the time I finished my hand was aching, and then I had to do my homework. Boy, was I tired after that! Before I got into bed I went downstairs with a flashlight and had another peek. The web glowed golden in the flashlight beam. I decided to call the spider Goldie.

The next day Julie came over after school. She sat on the swing chair and asked me riddles from a riddle book while I looked at Goldie.

"Why didn't the chicken cross the road?" Julie said.

"I don't know, why?"

"Because he was chicken!" Julie said, and chuckled. "Get it? He was — "

"I get it, I get it," I said. The leaves of the hanging plant were tickling my neck. I pushed them aside, but they brushed against my neck again. I turned around. Then I noticed some white blobs on the undersides of the leaves. I held the magnifying glass to them.

"Why was the cook cruel?" Julie said.

"Hey, Julie!" I called.

"Because she whipped the cream and beat the eggs," she said.

"Julie, come here!"

She crouched beside me. I pointed to the leaves of the plant. "You see those white things?"

"Yeah."

"You know what they are?"

"Cotton balls?"

"Nope. Egg sacs."

"Egg sacs?" she repeated.

"Yup." I grinned. "That means Goldie's going to have babies."

Julie put both hands over her heart and said, "How sweet. Little spider babies. Let's knit them some booties, what do you say? Little bitty pink and blue booties — "

"You goof," I said, pushing her shoulder. She fell over and lay on her back, saying, "With teeny weeny pom-poms — "

"Stop!" I yelled, laughing, and tickled her until she quit.

A few days later when I got home from school, there was a letter for me from the American Association of Arachnology. I tore it open and read:

Dear Ms. Shapiro:

What delightful news your letter brought, and what a fortunate young lady you are! The last time *Nephilia* was sighted in the Northern Hemisphere was ten years ago, and that was in a greenhouse, which hardly counts. I would concur with your Papaya Theory. And, although it cannot be proven, I would agree that the warm air from your mother's kiln is a major factor in the spider's survival. I pray that your mother has a great deal of pot-making planned in the near future.

I simply must see your *Nephilia*. Therefore, with your kind permission, I will arrive at your home at approximately 4:05 P.M. on Thursday the 11th. I will examine the spider and verify your identification. Please notify me at once if this is inconvenient.

> In arachnological friendship,
> *Morgan H. Grandview*
> President, AAOA

I called Julie and read the letter to her. "Arachnological friendship?" she said. "Are you kidding?"

"I thought it was sort of snappy," I said.

"Star, you're weird."

"Thanks a lot," I said. "Look, Julie, you've got to be here when he comes."

"Oh, no, I don't."

"Yes, you do."

"No, I don't."

"Do."

"Don't."

"Please!"

"Oh, OK." She started giggling. "What's the guy's name? Morgan T. Grandmarch?"

I giggled too. "Grandview. Morgan H. Grandview."

"Can't wait to meet him. See you, Star."

I hung up. Knowing that Julie would be with me made me feel good. I read the letter again. First sighting in ten years — wow!

Later I showed my mom and dad the letter. "Good for

you, Star," my dad said.

My mom smiled. "It just so happens I do have a lot of work lined up." She leaned forward with a serious look. "But remember our rule about keeping the spider out of the house."

"I will," I said. "Promise."

That night I lay in bed and thought, The president of the AAOA coming to my house — neat-o! Maybe I'll even get my name in the *Arach-news*! And my picture, too. I imagined a photographer taking pictures of me and Goldie. As I fell asleep I was saying, "Say cheese, Goldie."

Chapter Four

ON MONDAY morning there was a big cardboard box at the front of our classroom. It was almost as big as an oven. It was taped shut. FRAGILE was printed on the side. It smelled good. We were all dying to know what was in it, but Ms. Rooney wouldn't tell us. "After math," she said. Everybody groaned. Math is our last lesson in the afternoon!

All day we kept asking questions about the box and Ms. Rooney kept saying, "All good things come to those who wait." I thought math would never end. When Ms. Rooney told us to put our books away, we must have set a record for clearing off our desks. Then she sat on the edge of her desk. "I have some exciting news," she said, smiling. "Our class is going on a camping trip to Dogwood Lake."

Neat-o! I thought. I can use my new sleeping bag!

"Yahoo!" somebody yelled. Someone else called, "Yabba-dabba-doo!" and everyone laughed.

Ms. Rooney held up her hand for quiet. "We'll be staying in small cabins at the lake. We'll cook over a campfire. You can bring fishing gear."

Everybody started talking at once. "Wait till you see my new fishing rod!" Jimmy Tyler yelled.

"There's bears there," called Lucy Chatham.

"Can we pick who we sleep with?" Miranda asked.

I turned around and looked at Julie. She pointed to me and then to herself, as if to say, We'll sleep together. I nodded.

Ms. Rooney clapped her hands to quiet us down. "The

school board will pay for the bus, but not for the cabins. That means everyone has to bring in ten dollars," she said. "Now, I know that's a lot. But the mystery box may help you out." Smiling, she took a pair of scissors from her desk. "Sadie's Bakery on Fraser Street has kindly donated cookies for you to sell to raise money," she said, running the blade of the scissors along the tape. "Of course, you do not have to sell the cookies. You can ask your parents for the money or earn it some other way."

"I've got twenty-three dollars in my bank," Tommy Scott called out.

"Good, you can pay for me," Jimmy said quickly.

Everyone laughed. "For those of you who are less wealthy, selling cookies might be a fun way to raise the money," Ms. Rooney said, folding back the lid of the box. A delicious smell floated around the room. "Each box costs $1.25. Now, how many boxes will you have to sell to make $10.00?"

Everybody started trying to figure out the answer. "Six!" Tommy shouted. Ms. Rooney frowned and shook her head. "Seven!" someone else call out. Ms. Rooney frowned deeper. I traced the numbers on my desk with my finger. "Eight," I yelled, just a second before Miranda called out the same answer.

"Right," said Ms. Rooney.

Miranda gave me a dirty look. I ignored it.

"The money is due two weeks from Friday, along with any unsold cookies," Ms. Rooney said. "The trip is the next day, on Saturday. Any questions?"

"What kind of cookies are they?" Jimmy asked.

Everyone laughed, even Ms. Rooney. "An assortment," she said. Then she gave each of us a bag with eight boxes of cookies, a list of camping supplies, and an envelope for the money.

Julie and I got our bags and left. She had a funny look on her face. "What's the matter?" I said.

"I don't think my parents'll let me go," she said.

"Why not?"

"Well, they're so fussy about everything — and my grandparents are worse," she said. "They'll have to know how many parents are coming along and who's sleeping in which cabin and what we're having for breakfast and all that. If everything doesn't sound perfectly proper and safe, they'll say no." Her eyebrows were all wrinkled. "Do you think yours'll let you go?"

I nodded. "They're really into nature and camping and stuff." I was quiet for a minute. "There's only one thing."

"What?"

"They're definitely not into store-bought cookies."

"These are from the bakery," Julie said.

"That doesn't help. If they're not homemade or from Uprising Bakery, forget it."

We walked in silence. Julie sighed. "I really want to go," she said.

"Me, too." We walked on. When we reached the corner where we went different ways we wished each other good luck. I turned down my block. They'll let me, I said to myself. The cookies won't matter 'cause they'll want me to go camping.

When I got home I left the bag in the front hall and went into the kitchen. My mom and dad were in there, making whole wheat spaghetti. My dad mixed the eggs and flour and stuff in a bowl and dumped it into the pasta machine. My mom turned the handle and held a bowl to catch the spaghetti as it came out the other end.

"Hey, guess what!" I said. "Our class is going on a camp-

ing trip at Dogwood Lake. We're going to sleep in cabins and go fishing and stuff."

"Sounds like fun," my mom said.

"We have to bring in ten dollars," I said. "And you know something really nice? This — "

"Stah," Peggy called from the hall. "What dis?" She came into the kitchen, dragging the bag of cookies behind her.

"Peggy!" I yelled. I was going to break the news about the cookies nice and easy. Well, she'd ruined that plan. I took a deep breath. "So, well, one of the bakeries gave us cookies to sell and everybody got eight boxes and you have till two weeks from Friday to sell them and wasn't that nice of the bakery and boy, it'll sure be fun to go camping."

I stopped to catch my breath. My dad kept mixing dough and my mom kept turning the handle. "Cookies?" my dad said.

"From Uprising?" my mom said.

I shook my head.

"Forget it," they said together.

"But Mom — "

"Star, those cookies are made with white sugar and white flour and chemicals and all kinds of junk," my mom said.

"So?" I answered. "I'm not going to eat them."

"But you want to sell them to other people," my dad said.

"Right," I said. Good. It sounded like he understood.

He shook his head. "The end doesn't justify the means."

"What does that mean?" I said crossly.

"It means that even if the thing you're going to get in the end is wonderful, if the way you get it is wrong, then the whole thing is wrong," he said. "You see?"

"No, I don't," I said, stamping my foot.

My dad sat down on a chair and held out his arms. I stayed where I was. "Listen, honey, Mom and I believe that the way people eat affects the way they feel."

"So?"

"So, those cookies are unhealthy, right?"

I hesitated. "I guess so."

"So selling them to people would just add to the sickness in the world, which I'm sure you wouldn't want to do."

I put my hands on my hips. I didn't see what sickness in the world had to do with my camping trip. And I didn't care. "You don't understand," I said. "I need ten dollars. I don't have it. My piggy bank's empty from when I bought my magnifying glass, remember?"

My mom sat down on the other side of me. "Yes, I remember."

"So where am I going to get the money? Are you going to give it to me?"

My dad shook his head. "I don't think that would be appropriate."

I felt like we were going around in circles. "Well, that leaves the cookies," I said in a loud voice.

"Calm down, Star," my mom said. "Selling cookies is only one way to raise money. Maybe you can think of some other way."

"Like what?" I was practically yelling.

"Think about it for a while," my dad said. "You'll come up with something. You're creative."

"I am not!" I yelled. I hate being told I'm creative. I'm not. I don't have a great imagination. I don't have lots of ideas. I have a scientific mind, not a creative one.

I turned and looked at Peggy. She had taken a box of cookies out of the bag and was lifting the lid. "Don't touch that!" I yelled. I grabbed the box from her hands and ran upstairs.

I sat on my bed hugging my knees. How am I going to make ten dollars, I said to myself. Maybe I'll find a ten-dollar bill on the ground. I'd see it fall out of a lady's purse. I'd pick it up and run over to her. "Excuse me, you dropped this," I'd say. She'd say, "Oh, my, why so I did." Then she'd smile and say, "Just to reward you for your honesty, young lady, you may keep it. And thank you." I'd curtsy and say, "You're welcome." As I walked away, she'd say, "Now there's a fine example of youth for you."

But then I remembered that the most money I'd ever found was a nickel. Scratch that idea.

I thought some more. I thought of raking leaves. But at fifty cents a yard, I'd have to do twenty yards. Forget it. I'd never find twenty yards to rake.

Then I remembered that sometimes my parents paid me a quarter for folding the laundry. Twenty-five cents into ten dollars.... Forty loads of laundry. But our family didn't have that much dirty clothes in two and a half weeks — not even with Peggy. Maybe I could dirty some clothes on purpose, I thought. Yeah. I could fall down in the mud, splash paint on my shirt.... No. My mom and dad wouldn't appreciate that too much.

I sat there. I drummed my fingers on my leg. I cleaned my fingernails. I twisted a lock of hair round and round my pinky. I couldn't think of a thing. See, I said to my parents in my imagination, I told you I wasn't creative.

After supper I called Julie. I could tell from her voice that her parents had said yes. "How about you?" she said.

I told her about the ends and means. "I don't get it," she said.

"Neither do I," I said grumpily, then added, "It's a real switcheroo."

"What do you mean?"

"You thought your parents would say no, but they said yes. I thought mine would say yes, but they said — hey, wait a minute."

"What?"

"They didn't say I couldn't sell cookies. They just said I couldn't sell *those* cookies."

"So?"

"So if I had some other cookies — not sugary ones — I could sell them instead," I said.

"Yeah, but where are you going to get them?" Julie said.

"Make them."

"What?"

"Make my own," I said. "If they're healthy, my parents'll say OK. I think."

"We-ell-ll," Julie said thoughtfully. "It's worth a try, I guess."

"Hang on a sec," I said.

I laid down the phone and ran to the workshop. Just as I put my hand on the doorknob, I heard my mom make a strange noise. It sounded like "Whooo-eee!" combined with a laugh. Perfect timing, I said to myself. She just gave birth.

I went in. My mom was beaming at her pot and patting it like it was a baby. My dad was straightening up his work table, whistling as usual. I explained my idea. They both smiled. "Sounds fine to me," my dad said.

"Very creative thinking, Star," my mom added.

Aarrgghh! There was that word again.

I ran back to the phone. "They said OK."

"Great," Julie said. "I just have one question."

"What?"

"Do you know how to make cookies?"

"Well... no," I said. "But I figure we — "

"We? Who, me?"

"Yeah, you," I said. "We can just follow a regular cookie recipe and change the junky stuff to good stuff. Like, use whole wheat flour instead of white flour, like that."

"Is that how they make health food cookies?" Julie said.

"Sure," I answered. I really didn't know, but it made sense.

"OK, I'll help," Julie said.

"Tomorrow," I said, and we hung up.

The next morning I went to school early and returned the bakery cookies to Ms. Rooney. I told her I was going to try to raise the money another way. "Good for you," she said, then winked and added, "Good luck."

"Thanks," I said. I'll need it, I thought.

After school Julie and I went right to my house. I got a cookbook and turned to the chapter on desserts. We flipped through the pages. Pineapple upside-down cake... fudge brownies (my mouth watered at that one, but I kept turning)... apple pandowdy (Julie said that sounded like an apple with an old lady's face, wearing a flowery hat)... Finally we came to a recipe called Basic Drop Cookies. I looked over the ingredients: butter, sugar, eggs, flour, baking soda, vanilla. It looked simple and easy. At the bottom it said, "Makes 4 dozen."

"We'll have to make twice as much," I said, getting out one of my mom's bowls. It was big and wide and deep. On the outside the clay was carved to look like fish scales. On one side the bowl had a handle in the shape of a fish head, on the other a handle shaped like a tail. "My mom used to be into fish," I told Julie.

"Before dragons?" she said.

"Yeah." I got some measuring cups and spoons. "OK, ready," I said.

Julie read the recipe out loud. "One cup butter," she said.

"So that would be two cups," I said.

"Right."

"My mom says oil is healthier than butter," I said. I got the big container of oil. Julie held the measuring cup over the bowl while I tilted the container up. The first cup went OK, but the second time the oil came gushing out, filled the cup, and splashed over the sides. "That's OK," I said, "a little extra oil is good for you. What's next?"

"Two cups sugar. So, four cups."

I got the honey pot. "The nice thing about honey is that it's sweeter than sugar, so you don't have to use as much,"

I said. "So I'll just put in a little."

We went on through the recipe. Julie dropped an egg into the bowl and it smashed, but we fished out all the little bits of eggshell. At least, we tried to, but some of the littlest ones got buried in the dough and we couldn't find them. We put in whole wheat flour instead of white flour. I wasn't sure if baking soda was good for you, so we left it out. Then we added some wheat germ, soy grits, brewer's yeast, sunflower seeds, and carob powder for nutrition.

I took a small brown bottle down from the shelf. The label said Kelp Powder — Nature's Wonder Food from the Ocean. "Hey, this stuff is really good for you," I said. I meant to put in just one spoonful, but my hand jiggled.

Then we started mixing the dough. Boy, was it stiff! I stirred until my arm got tired, and then Julie took over. We took turns until we didn't see any more lumps of flour. We each dipped a finger in and scooped up some dough. It tasted — well, not too great.

Julie made a face. "Maybe we should put in some more honey."

I shook my head. "We don't want it to be too sweet."

"Star, you could probably dump the whole honey pot in there and it wouldn't be too sweet."

"Oh, come on," I said. "Remember, the cookies have to be healthy or I won't be allowed to sell them. Besides, you can't tell from the dough. Cookies always taste different when they're baked." I hoped they would taste different. Better.

When all the cookies were baked, I took one, broke it in half, and gave half to Julie. She ate her half and I ate mine. It tasted different from the dough, all right. Worse.

"I'm in trouble," I said.

Julie drank a glass of water. She looked at the counter

44

full of cookies and then at me. She began to giggle. They're awful," she said.

I began to giggle, too. "Terrible."

"Horrible."

We laughed harder.

"Disgusting," I said.

"Horrendous."

"What am I going to do?" I said, catching my breath.

"Don't worry," Julie said, hiccoughing, "Somebody'll buy them."

I gave her a look that said, You're nuts. "I hope so," I said.

We arranged that she'd come after school the next day and help me sell the cookies. Then she went home.

After supper I let my mom, dad, and Peggy try a cookie. They loved them. "Delicious!" my dad said. My mom said, "I can taste the nutrition." Peggy said, "Moah!"

Then I knew I was in trouble. If my family liked them, they must be lousy. But I put them in boxes, wrote HEALTH FOOD COOKIES — GOOD TO EAT AND GOOD FOR YOU — $1.25 on each box, and stacked them on the counter, ready for the next day.

Chapter Five

T HE NEXT day was bright and sunny. Yellow and orange leaves were falling from the trees and scuffling along the curbs. It seemed like a good day to sell health food cookies. Julie and I put the boxes in Peggy's little red wagon and went next door to the Wentworths'.

Mr. and Mrs. Wentworth are old. They give us vegetables from their garden. When they invite us over to help decorate their Christmas tree, they always let me climb on a ladder and put the star on top. "After all, her name *is* Starshine," Mrs. Wentworth says with a wink. Even though I'm sick of that joke, I smile anyway, because she's so nice.

I rang the doorbell. Mrs. Wentworth came to the door. "Oh, hello, Starshine," she said, smiling. "What can I do for you?"

"Well... um, would you like to buy some cookies? So I can go camping?"

Mrs. Wentworth put her hands on her hips. "Oh, what a shame!" she said. "You're too late. A little girl came over yesterday — sweet little thing with blond curls — and I bought two boxes from her."

Miranda. Wouldn't you know it?

"These ones are different," I said, opening a box and showing her. "They're homemade."

Mrs. Wentworth smiled as she shook her head. "Oh, dear me, no. Two boxes is more than enough for us. I'm sorry, honey. Next time you let me know you're selling, and I'll be sure to buy from you, OK?" She closed the door.

Julie and I turned the wagon around. "Fooey on Miranda," Julie said. I giggled. We pulled the wagon up the front walk of the next house. The Hoopers lived there. They were young. They rode bikes together. I knocked, and Mr. Hooper came to the door. "Hi, Starshine," he said.

I took a deep breath. "Hi, Mr. Hooper. My class is going on a camping trip — "

"Oh, how nice. Where to?"

"Dogwood Lake," I answered.

"Great place. You'll have a wonderful time."

"I know. I mean, I hope so," I said. "I'm selling cookies."

"Cookies?"

"To raise money."

"Money?"

"To go on the trip."

He thought for a moment. "Yes, I get it."

"So would you like to buy some?" I asked.

"Gee, I'd like to help you out, Starshine, but we try to stay away from sugar."

I showed him a box. "They're homemade. No sugar."

"Homemade, eh?" he said.

I took a cookie out of the box and broke off a corner. He put the piece in his mouth. As he chewed he sucked his cheeks in more and more and then swallowed with a big gulp. "You're absolutely right. Not a trace of sugar." He swallowed again. "I'm sorry, but uh — no thanks."

Julie and I turned down the front walk. "Don't worry," she said in a fake cheerful voice, "that's only two. Somebody'll buy."

I nodded my head. Sure they would. I only had to sell eight boxes. Eight dozen health food cookies. Eight times twelve... 96 cookies. Gosh, that was an awful lot of cookies to get rid of.

No one was home at the house next to the Hoopers. At the next house a woman came to the door wearing an apron, followed by two little boys. She had a pancake turner in her hand. The boys were holding cookies. When I told her about my cookies, she laughed and said, "Oh, my, I'm baking six dozen cookies myself! Thanks anyway."

As we walked away Julie said, "Mmmm, they smelled great. Think she'd trade a dozen of hers for a dozen of yours?" I punched her on the arm.

The next house was the last on the block. "You talk," I said to Julie as we climbed the front steps. She rang the doorbell. We waited a long time. It looked like no one was home. Just as we turned away, the door opened and a very old woman looked out. "Yes?" she said. She had silvery-white hair and a soft voice. She looked nice.

Julie explained about the cookies. The old woman smiled sadly. "Oh dear," she said, "two little boys came here the other day, and I just couldn't say no to them, so I bought a box from each one." She laughed softly. "It's just me in the house. I don't know how I'll ever eat all those cookies." She leaned forward. "Sorry, girls."

"That's OK," I said.

Julie and I walked to the corner and crossed the street. The wagon wheels went ka-bump, ka-bump down the curb and ka-bump, ka-bump up the curb on the other side. "Come on, now, give 'em a good smile," Julie said as we started up the first front walk. I showed my teeth. "Oh, that's great," Julie said, "real natural." I giggled. "That's better," she said.

A man came to the door. He said they never ate sweets, EVER, and slammed the door.

"You old crab," Julie said under her breath, and then we ran down the front walk in case he'd heard, jerking the wagon behind us.

I was beginning to get worried. We'd been to six houses and I hadn't sold a single cookie.

"I'll do the talking this time," Julie said as we came to the next house. An oldish woman answered the door. "*Bonjour, Madame,*" Julie said in a French accent, "we have some dee-leesh-ous cook-ees. *Les bonbons*, you know?"

I clenched my teeth so I wouldn't laugh. The woman looked confused. "Bonbons?" she said. Julie convinced her to try a bite. The woman chewed for a while. Then she turned her back to us and spit the chewed-up mush into a tissue. She turned back around. "No, thanks," she said, and closed the door.

Halfway down the front steps, we burst out laughing. "*Les bonbons?*" I said.

"Chewed up health food cookie mush," Julie said, holding her sides.

"Yuck," I said.

There were three more houses on the block. We got NO — no one home — NO. Silently we crossed the street. Up the next block and down the other side. Some of the people had already bought cookies from somebody in my class. Some said they didn't eat sweets. Some just said no. At the end of the second side I said, "I give up." Julie didn't say anything. We started walking home. We didn't talk. The only sounds were our footsteps and the rattling of the wagon. When we got to my house, Julie turned to me. "It was a good idea," she said.

"No, it wasn't," I said. "It was a crummy idea."

"No, it wasn't," she insisted, a little annoyed. "It was a good idea."

I let go of the wagon handle and it clanked to the ground. "Well, if it was such a good idea, why didn't it work? Huh?"

Julie put her hands on her hips. "I don't know why it didn't work. And you don't have to yell, either."

I turned away, folding my arms across my chest. I knew I didn't have to yell. But I felt rotten. What was I going to do? I'd done all this work, and I still had no money.

After a while Julie said, "What are you going to do with the cookies?"

"I don't know. Throw them out," I said in a grumpy voice. "No — my family'll eat them. My dumb family'll eat them."

Julie didn't say anything for a minute. Then she said, "Sorry it didn't work, Star. See you tomorrow." She headed down the walk. I watched her go. Then I took the eight boxes of cookies, dumped them on the kitchen counter, and went to my parents' workshop. My mom was bent over the potter's wheel. My dad was using his torch to melt the strips of lead that go between the pieces of glass. He had his goggles on and was whistling. They didn't hear me come in.

I slammed the door. My mom looked up. My dad turned his head, saw me, and turned off the torch. "Well?" my mom said.

I shoved my hands into my pockets. "Zero," I said.

"Zero?" my dad said.

"Zero. I didn't sell a single cookie."

"Gee, I can't understand it," my dad said, pushing the goggles back on his head. "Those cookies are delicious."

"*You* might think so," I said, "but nobody else does."

My mom pushed back a strand of hair, streaking it with orangey-brown clay. "It's a bummer, huh, Star?" I nodded. She beckoned with her finger and I went over to her. "Well, I don't know what's wrong with all those crazy people out there," she said, "but *we'll* buy a box of your cookies."

"$1.25. Big deal," I said.

"It's a start," my dad said, walking over.

"Yeah, all I need is — uh... eight seventy-five," I said. I swallowed down a lump in my throat. "Goodbye, camping trip."

"Nonsense," my dad said.

"You'll go," my mom said.

"But how?"

"You'll think of a way," my dad said.

"I did think of a way," I said, "and it didn't work."

"You'll think of another way," he replied.

I squished a small lump of clay with my shoe. "The only way I can think of is if you give me the money, and I pay you back out of my allowance."

They both shook their heads. "It's not the money, Star," my dad began, "it's the principle of the thing."

I groaned. "Not the ends and means again."

"Kind of," my mom said. "What we mean is, we want you to meet the challenge of earning the money to go on the trip."

"It's one of those lessons of life," my dad added.

I rolled my eyes. My parents are very big on lessons of life. Then I thought of something. "So is going camping," I pointed out.

"True," my mom said, "but it's not the same if you have

the money given to you."

"I don't care if I have it given to me or I rob a bank," I yelled.

"Star," my mom said, giving me a scolding look.

"Well, what am I supposed to do?" I shouted. "You won't let me sell the sugary cookies, the health food ones bombed — "

"Star," my dad interrupted softly. I looked at him. He ruffled my hair. "Don't get all upset. You've still got two weeks to figure it out."

"But — " I began.

"No buts," my mom cut in. "You've got $1.25 already. Surely you can think of a way to earn $8.75 in the next two weeks. You're creative."

There was that word again. I made fists. No, I'm not! I wanted to shout.

My dad reached out and pulled me to him. "We don't want to keep you from going camping, Star. We just want you to give it your best shot."

"See what you can come up with," my mom added. "We'll help if we can."

"Oh, OK," I said half-heartedly. I went to the kitchen and looked at the calendar. Today was Wednesday. The money was due two weeks from Friday. That gave me sixteen days. As I was counting on the calendar, I noticed that tomorrow was the 11th. That sounded like something. I tried to remember what. Somebody's birthday? No. A test? No. A dentist appointment? No.

Then I remembered. Mr. Grandview was coming. My stomach flip-flopped. I phoned Julie. "Mr. Grandview's coming tomorrow," I said.

"Who?"

"Morgan H. Grandview. You know, the guy from the

American Assciation of Arachnology."

"Oh, yeah." Julie giggled. "Yes, my de-ah," she said in her stuffiest accent, "Morgan H. Grandview at your sah-vice."

"Remember, you said you'd be here with me."

"What if I've changed my mind?"

"Julie!"

She laughed. "Don't have a bird. I'll be there."

I gave a sigh of relief. "OK. See you tomorrow."

Later that evening as I was going upstairs to bed, I heard my mom and dad talking in the living room. "Poor Star," my dad said.

I stopped on the second landing and listened.

"Yeah," my mom said, "she was really heartbroken about the cookies."

"I can't believe nobody bought any," he said.

"Me neither," my mom said. "I thought people were more health-conscious nowadays."

There was a long pause. "Say, Joanie," my dad began, "if she doesn't make the money — I mean, if she gives it a good try but comes up short, what do you say we make up the difference?"

Yay, Dad! I thought.

My mom didn't answer right away. I held my breath. Then she said, "I don't think we should. I want her to go camping just as much as you do. But it's the principle of the thing, like you said before. She's got to learn to draw on her own resources."

Draw on my own resources — that was a new one. I wondered if it was something like being creative.

"Yeah, I guess so," my dad said. "I'd just hate to see her miss the trip on account of a few dollars."

So would I, I thought.

"She won't miss it," my mom said. "She's clever. I'll bet she has something up her sleeve already."

I peeked into my sleeve. Nothing. You're wrong, I thought as I tiptoed the rest of the way upstairs. Wrong, wrong, wrong.

Chapter Six

O N THE way home from school Julie and I talked about what we thought Morgan H. Grandview would look like. I said tall and skinny with short hair and a moustache. Julie said short, fat and bald. We made a bet. Whoever was closest, the other would have to carry her books and lunch box home from school all next week.

When we got to my house my mom and dad were both in the workshop. Peggy was nowhere in sight. Julie and I went up to my room and played checkers. I was just about to double-jump her when the doorbell rang. I jumped up and ran downstairs, with Julie right behind me.

Morgan H. Grandview was short, thin, bald, and had a moustache. "It's a tie," I whispered to Julie. He was wearing the kind of glasses that are only the bottom half and was carrying a black doctor's bag. He looked at us over the tops of his glasses. "Ms. Shapiro?"

"That's me," I said. He put out his hand and we shook hands. "Call me Star," I told him.

"Star?"

"Short for Starshine."

He hesitated. Then he said, "Very well, uh... Star." He didn't seem like the nickname type.

I introduced Julie, then led them through the house to the porch. On the way I told Mr. Grandview that the spider had laid eggs.

"Indeed?" His eyebrows went up and his glasses rose on his nose. "Splendid."

When we got out to the porch Mr. Grandview unzipped

his doctor's bag and pulled out a monster magnifying glass. I mean, it was huge. Then we went over to the corner.

I noticed first. Goldie wasn't there.

A second later Julie noticed. We dropped to our knees. The web was dangling from the wall, ripped. Goldie definitely wasn't in it.

Mr. Grandview hadn't noticed yet. "Good stream of warm air. Splendid. Now, if you'll excuse me, girls, I'm most anxious to view our precious *Nephilia*," he said, squatting behind us.

"She – she isn't – " I gulped. "She's gone."

"Please move," Mr. Grandview said impatiently. "I'm – gone? No. Quite impossible. Surely you're joking. Really now, this is no time for pranks."

Julie and I backed up on our hands and knees like two babies going in reverse. Mr. Grandview fell onto his knees with a thud and leaned forward. He looked over the tops of his glasses, then pushed them back onto his forehead and peered closer. "This is certainly a *Nephilia* web," he said, lowering his glasses. "Unmistakable. Beyond doubt." He looked at me. "You're sure you've seen the spider. The actual arachnid." He said it like he thought I might have made the whole thing up.

"Of course I'm sure. She was there this morning. Honest. I checked before school. I always check before school. Right here. Right in that web – " I couldn't go on. I felt like I might burst out crying.

"I've seen her," Julie added. "Lots of times."

Mr. Grandview's shoulders slumped. "Dreadful. Most unfortunate," he said.

I leaned around him and looked behind the web, under the web, over the web. No Goldie. Then I remembered the eggs. I spun around on my knees. "Oh, look – the eggs are still here," I cried.

Mr. Grandview examined the egg sacs with his magnifying glass. He looked up and down the vines and on both sides of the leaves. "Excellent egg sacs. Utterly undisturbed," he said, nodding his head. "But the specimen's disappearance is most regrettable," he added, and his shoulders slumped again.

I was totally puzzled. Where could Goldie be? She couldn't just disappear like that. The way the web was ripped, it looked like something had snatched her out. But what? A bird? A toad? I pictured her vanishing down the throat of a fat brown toad, and shuddered. Then I thought maybe she'd got homesick and had crawled away, searching for the tropics. I sighed.

Mr. Grandview straightened up so suddenly that his glasses bounced on his nose. "We must not despair," he said, slapping his thigh. "We must search. We must find her. Search and find, girls, search and find!" He dropped onto his hands and knees and started crawling around the porch, peering over his glasses.

I looked at Julie. She gave me a silly smile, as if to say, This is nuts — but I'll do it anyway. Then she began to crawl around. I sat there. I felt like crying. But we *had* to find Goldie. There was nothing to do but crawl. So I did.

We looked between cracks and under chairs. We looked over railings and under railings. We took apart dustballs and looked behind toys. "Here, Goldie, here, girl," I called.

Mr. Grandview looked up. "Goldie?"

"Yeah, well — you know, golden web...Goldie...." I blushed, expecting him to say, "How dreadfully silly," or something like that. But he didn't. He nodded his head several times and said, "Goldie. Yes. I get it. Very clever." Maybe he *was* the nickname type, after all.

We continued crawling around. Our hands and knees got filthy. All of a sudden Mr. Grandview said, "Wait! Could that be —" He lurched forward and bumped into a pile of firewood that was stacked in the corner. "Ooof!" he yelled, as the whole pile tumbled down.

The crash brought my mom running to the back door. "Star, are you OK?" Then, seeing the three of us on the floor, she said, "What's going on?"

"Mom, this is Mr. Grandview," I said. "Remember? The president —"

"Oh, yes," my mom said, walking over to him. She was in her work apron. Her face was streaked with clay and her hands were coated with the stuff. She held out her hand, then said, "Oh, sorry." She wiped it on her apron and held it out again. "How do you do?" she said. "I'm Joan Shapiro."

Mr. Grandview reached up and shook her hand with two of his fingers. "How do you do," he said.

My mom looked back at me. "Star, if you don't mind my asking...?"

"Goldie's missing," I said.

For a few seconds my mom just stood there, as if she hadn't heard. Then she dashed to the kitchen door and shouted, "Pete! Come on out back! Emergency!" She started crawling around with us. A minute later my dad stepped onto the porch, wearing his goggles. He turned his head from side to side. "Joanie? Where are you?" Then he saw us. "What — ?"

"Goldie's gone," my mom said.

"Goldie? Oh, Goldie," my dad said. He pushed the goggles back on his head and joined the search, whistling "The Eensy Beensy Spider." I was glad my mom and dad were helping. Even though they hated spiders, they cared about me. That made me feel a little better.

We all kept crawling around the porch. It's not a very big porch. We kept bumping into each other and saying things like, "Hey! What's that?"

"Just a piece of dirt."

"Ow, I got a splinter."

"Wait. I think — No, it's not."

"Hey, get your knee off my hand."

When we had gone over every inch of the porch at least fifty times, we all knew Goldie wasn't there. Everybody crawled slower. My dad even stopped whistling. My eyes filled with tears.

Mr. Grandview slowly stood up. He whisked the dirt off his knees, brushed his hands, and tucked in his shirt. He put his magnifying glass back in the doctor's bag and zipped it up. "Well, my dear, I see no point in continuing," he said.

I wished a hole would appear in the porch floor and I'd fall through. I couldn't say a word.

"Most regrettable," he added. "Unfortunate. Distressing."

"Mr. Gr — Grandview," I stammered, standing up. "She was there this morning. Honest."

He smiled sadly. "I do not doubt your word, Star." He sighed. "Such a rare opportunity." He looked over his shoulder, brightening a little. "At least there are the eggs." He picked up his black bag and turned toward Julie, my mom and my dad, who were still on the floor. "Nice to have made your acquaintance," he said with a nod of the head, then walked into the house. I followed him. Pausing in the front doorway, he said, "Please inform me when the eggs hatch," but he sounded as if he didn't expect me to. He shook my hand and walked down the front steps.

Just then Peggy came out of her room, "Look at me,

Stah," she said.

"Leave me alone, Peggy," I said in a grumpy voice.

"I'm not Peggy," she said, coming closer. She had on one of my mom's white slips, all bunched up at the waist so she wouldn't trip on it, and a ruffly bonnet thing on her head. She was holding a shoe box full of grass and leaves. "I'm Ittle Miss Muffet," she said.

"Who cares?" I replied.

She ignored that and began to recite in a sing-song voice, "Ittle Miss Muffet, Sat on a tuffet — "

I had a brainstorm. I grabbed the shoe box. Poking out from under a leaf were two brown hairy legs. I shrieked. Tucking the shoe box under one arm, I raced down the front steps, yelling, "Mr. Grandview! Mr. Grandview!"

Peggy ran after me in her slip and bonnet, shouting, "Gimme back! Dat's mine!"

I caught sight of Mr. Grandview just as he reached the corner. "Mr. Grandview!" I yelled again. He turned. I ran to him. Behind me Peggy was screaming, "Gimme!" and behind her I heard my parents and Julie calling, "What is it? What's going on?"

Panting for breath, I handed Mr. Grandview the shoe box. A look of amazement came over his face, then delight, then sadness. I looked in the box and saw why. Goldie was perfectly still. Dead. I burst out crying, right in the middle of the sidewalk. Mr. Grandview looked like he was strugling not to cry, too. "Such a shame," he said in a low voice. I blubbered harder.

My mom, dad and Julie caught up with us. Mr. Grandview held out the shoe box and showed them.

"Oh, gee," my dad said.

"Gimme," Peggy said, reaching for the box. "I want it."

"Be quiet!" I yelled. "It's all your fault!"

She threw herself on the grass and started screaming and kicking. "Dat's mine! Waaaahh!"

"She didn't mean to," my mom said to me, then knelt beside Peggy. "Now, Pumpkin — "

"Oh, my," Mr. Grandview said, then louder, "Oh, my!"

I looked at him. He was staring into the shoe box with a surprised look on his face. I peeked in. A leg was moving. Two legs. Gently he pushed away the grass and leaves. All of Goldie was wiggling, and she gave me a look as if to say, What's all the fuss about?

"She's alive!" I yelled. Peggy stopped screaming. Everyone crowded around.

"A magnificent specimen," Mr. Grandview said as I hugged Julie. "Apparently unharmed. Oh, how splendid.

Simply marvelous."

I carried the shoe box back to the porch. Mr. Grandview looked at Goldie with all eight magnifying glasses in his bag. Then he very gently put her back in the corner. He said she'd fix up her web and she'd be all right *if* — he looked right at Peggy — she were left alone. Peggy didn't hear. She was too busy saying, "Ittle Miss Muffet."

Then we all went inside for tea. My mom put some of my health food cookies on a plate. "Have a cookie?" she said to Mr. Grandview.

"Star made them," my dad said, taking one.

"And Julie," I said quickly. I didn't want all the blame.

"No, thanks," Mr. Grandview said, "I don't eat sweets."

"Don't worry, they're not sweet," I said under my breath.

Mr. Grandview raised his eyebrows. "Well, in that case, I just might try one," he said, reaching for a cookie.

Oh no, I thought. We've already had enough trouble today.

"Mmmm," he said. "Mmmmmmmm."

I looked at him. He wasn't joking. "Delicious. Quite delicious," he said, popping the rest of the cookie into his mouth and reaching for another. "May I?"

I couldn't believe it. I'd thought all along he was a little strange. Now I knew it.

"Have as many as you like," my dad said to Mr. Grandview, pushing the plate closer to him. "We've got eight dozen."

Mr. Grandview looked at him over the tops of his glasses. "Eight dozen?"

I explained about the camping trip. "Since you have such a substantial surplus," Mr. Grandview said, "I'd be most obliged if you'd allow me to purchase a box. My wife and I enjoy a little something with our tea."

"Uh...sure," I said. I got a box of cookies from the pile and gave it to him.

"Splendid," he said, handing me a dollar and a quarter.

Well, now I had two dollars and fifty cents. Only seven-fifty to go. Only.

Before he left, Mr. Grandview told me the eggs'd probably take a few more weeks to hatch. He also said that arachnologists almost never had the opportunity to observe tropical spiders in British Columbia, so it was very important for me to note the exact time and day the eggs hatched, and let him know right away. I promised I would.

After he left, I got a piece of paper. At the top I printed NEPHILIA BABIES, and then, along the side, just like we number our papers for a spelling test, I wrote   DATE
                                                          TIME.
Then I added WEATHER just to be sure.

I stuck the paper to the porch wall with thumb tacks and put a pencil in a little crack between two of the wall boards. I checked the egg sacs to see if anything was happening. Nothing was. They looked as cottony and blobby as ever. "Well, I'm ready whenever you are," I told them.

After supper I told Peggy in my bossiest voice not to touch the spider again. Ever. She smiled at me. "I'm not Ittle Miss Muffet anymore. I'm Ittle Bo Beep now." I didn't know whether to hug her or strangle her.

Chapter Seven

O N THE way to school the next day I got an idea for raising the money. A super idea. I was so excited, I rode my bike a block past the school yard before I realized where I was. I rode back and played hopscotch, waiting for Julie. I was on fivesies when she pedaled into the school yard.

"Julie, I know how to raise the money!"

"How?" she said, locking her bike.

"A spider museum."

She looked at me. "A what?"

"A spider museum. I'd gather a bunch of spiders, see. All different kinds. Like, a few gardens, a nursery web or two, a daddy longlegs. Of course there's Goldie, too. I'd put them in jars — "

"Star — "

"Don't worry, I'd punch holes in the top."

"I don't think — " Julie began.

"There is one problem," I said.

"What's that?" Julie asked.

"Food."

"Food?" she repeated.

"Yeah. It has to be alive."

"How come?"

"'Cause spiders catch their food by vibration. Like, they kind of feel an insect moving, and then they pounce. They don't go for dead bugs."

She made a face. "Ugh."

"Well, I'll figure that out later," I said. "But anyway,

I'll put up signs explaining what the spiders are and where they live and what they eat and — "

"Star," Julie interrupted.

"Yeah?"

"What does all this have to do with the camping trip?"

I looked at her like she was being really thick. "Don't you see? I'll charge people to come to the museum. Say, a dime or a quarter — "

"Star, I don't think — "

"I'll let them go after," I added.

"Who, the people?"

"No, the spiders, silly. It isn't right to keep them, you know."

"You're nuts," she said. "No one is going to pay you to look at spiders."

"I'll even let them use my magnifying glass — if they promise to be careful."

"Star, forget it. People don't like spiders. They're afraid of them."

"They'll be in jars," I pointed out. "Except Goldie. I couldn't put her in a jar."

Julie put her hand on my shoulder. "Star, I hate to tell you this, but you're not going to make $7.50 with a spider museum."

"Why not?"

"'Cause people won't pay to see something they think is yucky."

"Spiders are not yucky!"

"To you they're not," she said. "To most people they are."

"But — " I began. Then I remembered what had happened in grade three. And how I'd been trying to get my mom and dad to like spiders for years, but they still didn't.

Julie was right. No one would come to the museum. It wouldn't work. I sighed. The school bell rang. We started walking toward the school. "There's only one thing I can do, then," I said in a low voice.

"What?"

I kicked a pebble. "Sell my magnifying glass."

Julie turned to me, hands on hips. "After you saved all that money for it?"

I kicked the same pebble. It rolled to the side. I kicked another. "Then what am I going to do?"

We squeezed into the crowd of kids pushing to get in the door. "We'll think of something," Julie said.

I didn't say anything. What else could I do, but sell my magnifying glass? It'd give me enough money to go on the trip, and some left over. I hated the thought — especially now, with Goldie to look at. No, I won't sell it, I said to myself. Unless I absolutely have to.

As I walked down the aisle to my seat, Miranda gave me one of her phony smiles. Normally I'd give her a phony smile back, just to keep things even, but today I didn't feel like it. I was mad at her for selling cookies to Mrs. Wentworth. Miranda knows where I live. She knew I had dibs on my next-door neighbor. But she went there anyway. Deep down I knew that even if she hadn't, and Mrs. Wentworth had bought a couple of boxes from me, it wouldn't have made much difference. I still wouldn't have enough money. But I was mad at her anyway. I gave her a dirty look and sat down at my desk.

Ms. Rooney came in carrying a huge stack of books. "Good morning," she said, dropping them on her desk, then turned to the class. "How are the cookie sales going?"

"Great!" everybody yelled. Except me. I slid down in my seat.

Ms. Rooney sat on the edge of her desk. She put her fingertips together and apart, together and apart, like she always does when she's got something interesting to tell us. "Has anyone heard of Charlotte Feldenstock?" she said.

The class was silent.

Ms. Rooney smiled. "Charlotte Feldenstock was the librarian here at Priscilla Marpole Elementary for about twenty-five years," she said. "Many of your mothers and fathers probably knew her when they attended this school. She died a few months ago."

I listened carefully. "Mrs. Feldenstock was a wonderful librarian," Ms. Rooney continued. "There must be hundreds of boys and girls who love to read because of her."

I pictured Charlotte Feldenstock looking like my grandma, my mom's mom. She's short and wrinkled and loves to read.

"Charlotte Feldenstock loved the myths of ancient Greece," Ms. Rooney said. "She used to say that the myths are just as true today as when they were first told, thousands of years ago." She walked across the front of the room. "In Mrs. Feldenstock's will, she set up an endowment for our school. An endowment is a gift of money. Mrs. Feldenstock's endowment is in the form of a contest."

I couldn't figure out what this contest and endowment were all about. I leaned forward on my desk.

"The contest is called The Myths Come Alive," Ms. Rooney went on. "It's open to everyone in the school. The idea is to learn about a myth, any myth, and then present it in some way." She ticked off the ways on her fingers. "You can tell the myth, or make a poster or painting or collage about it. You can recite an original poem about your myth, or sing an original song, or do a play, or write a book report, or make a model." She looked at her fingers. "That's nine ways. I'm sure you can come up with others. The school will have an assembly where all the classes will present their myths, and judges will choose winners in each grade."

"What's the prize?" Julie asked.

"A five dollar cheque and a copy of *Bullfinch's Mythology* for each grade level," Ms. Rooney replied.

"What's *Bullfinch's Mythology*?" Lucy Chatham asked.

"It's a book," Ms. Rooney said, "containing all the Roman and Norse myths, as well as the Greek ones."

I didn't care about *Bullfinch's Mythology*. I cared about the five dollar cheque. If I won, I'd have $7.50. I'd only need $2.50. Then I thought of something else. I'd get two allowances before the money for the camping trip was due. That would be two dollars more. So if I won, I'd have $9.50. I'd only be 50 cents short. My heart beat fast.

"Do we have to enter?" asked Tommy Scott.

"No," Ms. Rooney answered with a sly smile.

"Good," Tommy muttered.

"You can do extra social studies assignments instead," Ms. Rooney added.

Tommy and some of the other kids groaned.

"You may work by yourselves or in groups of two or three. Of course, if your group wins, you'll have to divide the prize," Ms. Rooney said. She pointed to a calendar hanging on the wall. "The contest is on Thursday, the 25th. That's a week from next Thursday."

"So soon!" Miranda said. For once I agreed with her.

"Yes, I know," Ms. Rooney said. "But I think you can all come up with a good entry by then." She pointed to the stack of books on her desk. "All of these are about the Greek myths. You may have the rest of the reading period to look at them and get ideas. Remember, the more imaginative your entry, the better your chance of winning." She passed out the books. But I didn't take one because I already knew what myth I was going to use — Arachne, of course.

I rested my chin on my hands and thought about how to present the story of Arachne. I definitely wasn't going to get up in front of the whole school and perform, so that got rid of telling it, reciting a poem about it, singing a song, and doing a play. What was left? Poster, painting, collage, book report, or model. I thought hard. The easiest thing to do would be to draw a big picture of Arachne and Athena and their weaving and all. But then I remembered a Cinderella poster I'd made in grade two. The teacher thought Cinderella was Drizella, and the fairy godmother was the stepmother. Maybe drawing a picture wasn't the best plan for me.

I thought some more. Finally I decided to write out the

story of Arachne on a big poster. I'd do it in my very best handwriting. I'd jazz it up by drawing little pictures around the edges. I sighed. My idea wasn't too thrilling. But maybe if I did a real special job, I'd have a chance.

"Excuse me, class," Ms. Rooney called. I looked up. She was hanging a piece of paper on the bulletin board with a thumb tack. "This is a sign-up sheet for the contest. Please sign up when you've decided which myth you're going to do. And if you choose not to enter, just put 'social studies' next to your name."

Everyone laughed. No one — not even Tommy — was going to choose that.

When the recess bell rang, Julie scurried up to my desk. "Well?" she said.

"Well, what?"

"What myth are you doing?"

"Arachne," I said. "How about you?"

"Either the Golden Fleece or Persephone," she said. "I can't decide."

We got our snacks and skipping ropes and went outside. It was a cold, sunny day. Brown leaves were scuffling around the school yard in the breeze. "What are you going to do with it?" Julie asked.

"Make a poster," I said, my mouth full of granola bar.

"Oh, Star," Julie said.

I looked at her. "What do you mean, 'Oh, Star'?" I took another bite.

"You've got to win this contest. You need the money."

"I know," I said, annoyed.

"Well, you're not going to with a poster," Julie said.

"Why not?"

"'Cause it's not exciting enough. You heard what Ms. Rooney said — the more imaginative your entry, the better chance you have of winning. And I hate to tell you, but you're not that great of an artist."

"I know that," I said in a hurt tone of voice. "I wasn't going to draw it, I was going to print it, for your information."

"That's even more boring," Julie said. I must have looked insulted, because she took my hand and said, "I'm not trying to hurt your feelings, Star."

"Well, you're doing a pretty good job," I said. I pulled my hand away and started jumping rope.

"I'm just trying to help you. I really want you to win."

I stopped jumping. "Why?"

" 'Cause if you don't go on the camping trip, I might have to sleep next to Miranda," Julie answered.

I laughed in spite of my hurt feelings.

"How about if we do something together?" she said, looking at me out of the corner of her eye.

"About Arachne?"

"Sure."

"OK," I said. "What'll we do?"

"How about a poem?"

I shook my head. "There's not many words that rhyme with Arachne."

"True," Julie said. She jumped pepper twenty-five times, then gave me another sideways look. "We could make up a song."

"Forget it," I said.

"Songs are real catchy," she pointed out.

"Julie, there is no way I'm going to get up in front of the school and sing."

"I'll sing with you," she said.

I turned to her, holding my skipping rope in my hand. "You see this rope? If I hear the word 'sing' one more time,

I'm going to wrap it around your neck."

"But, Star — "

"And squeeze," I added.

"But — "

"Hard."

Julie laughed. "OK, OK, I can see you're not into si — uh, music."

"Gee, whatever gave you that idea?" I said.

"It's got to be something different, that nobody else is doing," Julie said. A gust of wind picked up a bunch of leaves and swirled them around our feet. Suddenly she turned to me. "I've got it."

"What?"

"A play. We'll act out the story of Arachne."

"I can't act!" I said.

"Don't be silly," she replied. "Anybody can act."

"Not me," I said, shaking my head.

"Sure you can."

"You're nuts."

"No, I'm not. Remember the first time I came over, and you told me the story of Arachne?"

I nodded. How could I have forgotten that day?

"Well, you were acting then, sort of," Julie said.

"I was?"

"Mmm-hmm. The way you told it, you got me right into the story."

"I did?" I said.

"Yeah," Julie said. "I even got goose bumps."

"But that was different. It was just you. I couldn't act in front of the whole school."

"Why not?" Julie said. "It doesn't matter how many people are watching. You just say your lines, that's all."

"That's easy for you to say," I said. "You're good at

acting. You've done it lots of times. I haven't. It's not — it's not my thing."

"Well, what is your thing, then?" Julie said, slightly annoyed.

"Spiders. Looking at things under a magnifying glass."

"Well, you'll have lots of time to look at spiders while everybody else is at Dogwood Lake," she said.

"Julie — "

The school bell rang. We headed for the door. "It's up to you," Julie said. "If you don't want to do a play, fine. I'll do something myself."

"I'll think it over," I said.

Chapter Eight

I DID THINK it over — all through spelling. Deep down I knew Julie was right — a poster just wasn't exciting enough to win the contest. And I wanted to win. I *had* to win.

While Ms. Rooney talked about dividing words into syllables, I had a wonderful daydream. The contest judges called me up to the front of a huge crowd of people. Everyone was clapping and cheering. "Congratulations, Starshine," the judges said, handing me the cheque. I smiled and thanked them, waving to the people. Then, I got my new sleeping bag and climbed onto the bus for Dogwood Lake.

But then I thought of the play. My stomach knotted up, and I went into another daydream. I was standing in front of the audience with my mouth open and nothing coming out. Julie poked me with her elbow. "Come on, Star," she whispered, "it's your line." I couldn't think of it. My face got redder and redder, my mind got blanker and blanker.... I shook my head to get rid of the picture. Forget it, I said to myself. Some people can act and some people can't. I can't.

All day: up-down, yes-no, should-shouldn't. By the time school was over, I was totally mixed up. When I got home, I told my mom and dad about the endowment and the contest. "If I win, I'll have just about enough money for the camping trip," I said.

My mom smiled. "Isn't it amazing how things work out?"

"Yeah, but first I have to win," I said. I paused, then

said, "I thought I'd write out the story of Arachne on a big piece of paper and decorate it with pictures and stuff."

"That sounds nice," my dad said. He didn't sound thrilled.

"Julie says a poster's not exciting enough to win," I said quietly.

"That Julie's a smart cookie," my mom said.

"Don't use that word," I said.

"Oh. Sorry."

"She says I need something snappier to win. Like a play."

"She's right," my dad said. "A play would have a much better chance of winning than a poster."

"Yeah, but I can't act," I said.

"What do you mean, you can't act?" my mom said in a surprised voice. "You're always acting out little stories for Peggy."

"Yeah, but that's different. It's just Peggy. If I make a mistake or do something stupid, she doesn't know the difference. This would be in front of the whole school."

My dad put his hand on my leg. His eyes were twinkling. "I have news for you, Star. Mom and I have watched you a few times while you were doing those plays for Peggy."

"You have?" I said. My cheeks got warm.

"Mmm-hmm. And you know what? You were acting."

"I was?"

"Sure," my mom said. "You became different characters, and used different voices and gestures for each one. That's acting."

"Oh," I said. A tingle ran up my back.

"I think Julie's right," my dad said. "Go for the play."

"We could help make costumes or props," my mom said.

"Or help you learn your lines," my dad added.

I pulled my knees to my chest. "It's scary," I said in a low voice.

"Of course it is," my dad said. "Trying new things always is. But you can do it, I know you can. Besides, nothing ventured, nothing gained."

"What?" I said.

"Dad means if you don't try, you'll never have a chance of succeeding," my mom explained. "If you give up before you even start, you'll never know if you could have done it or not."

I thought about that and got even more mixed up. "Oh, I don't know," I said. I went out to the back porch, crouched down, and watched Goldie spin. "Listen, Goldie," I said, "if I do the play with Julie I'll probably make a fool of myself 'cause I don't know anything about acting. Not just in front of my class, but the whole school. But we might win. Probably not, but maybe. But if I do a poster, I won't win 'cause it's not exciting enough. But it's not scary, either." I paused. "What do *you* think, Goldie?" She didn't answer, just kept spinning. I leaned closer. "If I don't do the play, am I giving up before I even start? She stopped for a second, as if she was thinking about it. Then she went on spinning.

Watching her move across the web, I imagined she was Arachne, changed into a spider by Athena. She probably felt ashamed of her strange new body, and angry that Athena had punished her just because her weaving was better. She deserved to win. But maybe she was glad to be changed into a spider, 'cause then she could do what she loved to do. It was such a neat story. It didn't have a happily-ever-after ending, but it always gave me goose bumps. I looked at my arms. Sure enough, they were covered with goose bumps.

Goldie finished spinning and sat quietly in the middle of the web. What was it my dad had said — nothing ventured, nothing gained? However it went, it was true. If I didn't try the play, I wouldn't have a chance of winning. If I did try the play, I still might not win. But at least I'd have a chance.

Was it worth a try? Was it worth making a fool of myself? I stood up. Yes. I had to try. "There's worse things than making a fool of yourself," I told Goldie, "though I can't think of any at the moment."

I went into the living room. "I'll give it a try," I said.

"Good for you, Star," my dad said.

"That's the spirit," my mom added.

I smiled. I felt good — but scared, too. I phoned Julie and told her.

"All right!" she said.

"But if this thing bombs, I'm going to tell everybody it was your idea."

"It won't bomb, silly," she said. "It'll be fun."

"Fun?" I repeated. "You want to know what's fun?"

"What?"

"What's fun is to go for a walk in a field and find a big spider's web stretched across the grass. And you just happen to have your magnifying glass in your back pocket, so you take it out and you can see every thread and every drop of water and every one of the spider's eyes. That's fun."

"Star?" Julie said.

"Yeah?"

"You're weird."

"I am not," I said, beginning to laugh.

"But I love you anyway," she added. "Now, listen. Just in case you said yes, I thought up a bunch of titles for the play. Want to hear them?"

"OK."

She cleared her throat. "The Story of Arachne, The Ancient Myth of Arachne, The Maiden and the Goddess, The Wonderful World of Weaving — that's my favorite — The Contest Between Arachne and Athena, and Why Spiders Spin Webs. What do you like best?"

"The Wonderful World of Weaving?" I said. "Sounds like a Walt Disney show." I pretended the telephone was a microphone. "Welcome, boys and girls, to the wild, wacky, wonderful world of weaving."

Julie laughed. "Well, which one do you vote for?"

"The Story of Arachne," I said.

"Oh, dullsville," she said.

"Well, that's what it is," I said.

"I know, I know," Julie replied. "OK, The Story of

Arachne. I'll come over tomorrow and we'll start writing it."

Only she didn't come over. She called in the morning and said she'd caught a cold and had to stay in bed. I have to admit I was relieved that we weren't going to start working on the play. I went upstairs and put my allowance in my piggy bank. Now I had $3.50. Next week I'd have $4.50. And then...maybe...I wouldn't let myself think about it.

On Monday Julie was better, and came to school. Her face was pale and under her nose it was all red from wiping. She sounded like she had a clothespin on her nose. But I was glad she was there, because we were going to sign up to do the play, and without her I probably would have chickened out.

I checked the sign-up list to see what the other kids were doing. Miranda was going to tell about Aphrodite, The Goddess of Love. Yuck. Lucy Chatham had put Persephone — poem.

Tommy and Jimmy were in line behind us at the bulletin board. As I signed up for Julie and me, they kept pushing and bumping us. "Come on, come on, don't take all day." Jimmy said.

Julie turned around and gave him her dirtiest look. He put his hands to his face. "Oh, I'm so scared," he said.

Julie ignored it. Taking our time, we moved out of the way. Jimmy and Tommy moved forward. Tommy hooted. "Uh-ratch-nuh. Hey, Jimmy, look at this — Uh-ratch-nuh!"

"Uh-ratch-nuh, scratch-nuh," Jimmy said in a singsong voice.

"Hey, scratch me, Uh-ratch-nee!" Tommy yelled.

"It's not — " I began.

Julie took my arm. "Don't pay any attention to them," she said. "They just want to make us mad."

"They did," I said. But just then Ms. Rooney came in, and they stopped teasing. At reading period she let us work on our myths. I pulled a chair up to Julie's desk. She took a tissue out of her pocket and blew her nose. It looked so red and sore, I really felt sorry for her. "OK," she said, "let's start writing the play. I guess we'll start with you weaving."

"You mean *you* weaving."

"What do you mean, me weaving?" she said.

"Well, you're Arachne, so you'll be weaving," I said. "I'm Athena. I come in later."

Julie shook her head. Her black hair swung back and forth. "Unh-unh. You're Arachne."

"But Arachne's the biggest part."

"Right. So?"

"So!" I yelled. A few kids turned around. I leaned close to her and whispered, "Julie, I can't act! You're the one who knows all about acting. You should have the biggest part."

She shook her head again. "Arachne is your story, Star. You're the spider freak. You should be Arachne."

"But — oh, all right," I said. "I'll be Arachne." I shook my finger in her face and said, "If I blow this, I'll never speak to you again."

Julie grinned. "Guess what — you're a great actress already."

I gave her *my* dirtiest look.

"Now, come on," she said. "You have to tell them you're a poor peasant girl."

"What are they going to think I am, an elephant?"

"You never know," she said.

I kicked her under the desk. "OK, not an elephant," she said with a giggle. "A hippo."

I kicked her again. Only I missed, and banged my foot against the metal bar at the bottom of the desk. "Ow," I said. Julie giggled again. I giggled, too.

"Come on," she said. "How about 'I am Arachne, a peasant girl'?"

"OK. Now, she has to say she's poor," I said.

"Why? Is that important?"

"I don't know," I said. "But in the story it always says her family was poor."

"OK."

"So put 'I come from a poor family,'" I said.

Julie did, then looked at me and said, "But I am a terrific weaver."

"Not just a terrific weaver," I said, "the best weaver in all of Greece."

Julie wrote down "The best weaver in all of Greece" just the way I said it. She smiled at me. "Now, that wasn't so hard, was it?"

"Well, no," I admitted.

Julie opened her mouth, but before she could speak, I said, "If you say 'I told you so,' I'll — I'll stuff your mouth with tissues."

"Who, me?" she said, spreading her hands palm-up.

"Dirty ones," I said.

"Star," she said, putting her hand on my arm, "I wouldn't dream of saying, 'I told you so.'"

"You —"

The recess bell rang. "Saved by the bell," Julie said.

Chapter Nine

WHEN I got home from school, I went to the workshop to say hi to my mom. She was working on a big dragon pot shaped kind of like a vase but with a wide top. She was humming to herself so I knew it was OK to talk.

"What's that, Mom?"

"A dragon vessel," she answered.

"Like a ship, you mean?" It didn't look like it would float.

She smiled at me. "Not that kind of vessel. A vessel can also be a container or pot."

"Like, for granola or cookies or something?"

"Mmm-hmm. Or other things, like magic spells and dragon's breath." She lifted her eyebrows and gave me a funny smile. I never know when she's joking about stuff like that. I think she wants to believe in it. Sometimes I do, too. Sometimes I don't. I smiled back.

"How was school?" she said, turning the dragon around and beginning to shape its head.

"OK," I said. "Julie and I started working on the play."

"How'd it go?"

"Pretty good. We wrote four lines," I said.

"Let's hear them," my mom said.

"Aw, Mom...."

"Come on. You've got to practice anyway," she said.

"I don't know if I remember them," I said. That was a lie. I remembered them perfectly.

"Try," she said.

"Oh, OK," I said. "I am Arachne, a peasant girl. I come from a poor family. But I am a terrific weaver. The best

weaver in all of Greece."

My mom stopped working and smiled at me. "Terrific! Now, once more, with feeling."

"But Mom, this is only a practice — "

"That doesn't matter," she interrupted. "Come on, now, like you really mean it."

I hesitated. "Oh, all right," I said. I stood up straight and tried to pretend I was Arachne. I felt pretty silly. "I am Arachne, a peasant girl," I said loudly. For a second I could kind of see the green hillsides out of the corners of my eyes. "I come from a poor family." I said the rest in the same loud voice.

"Much better!" my mom said, grinning. "That time you were acting."

I smiled. I had felt it — just a bit. Maybe — just maybe — I could pull it off.

The next day Ms. Rooney again gave us the reading period to work on the contest. Julie and I were just about to get started when Ms. Rooney said, "I need someone to take a message to Mr. Horne in the grade two room."

Immediately most of the kids started jumping out of their seats and waving their arms like they were trying to wave them off and calling, "Me! Me!" I just sat there. I've learned that most teachers pass over the arm-wavers and pick somebody who sits quietly. Not always, but usually. Sure enough, Ms. Rooney nodded in my direction. "Starshine?"

I stood up, trying not to smirk, then took the slip of paper from her and left the room. I made the walk last as long as I could, walking one footstep to each square. While Mr. Horne was reading the paper, I looked at the grade twos. They looked so little. I couldn't believe I was that small just two years ago. Mr. Horne gave me a message for Ms. Rooney and I walked back to my room two steps to a square.

When I joined Julie again, she handed me some new lines she'd written. "Forsooth! Maiden Arachne is boasting she can weave better than me," I read to myself. Then, "Hark! How dare she say that? She forgets I am a goddess. I will have to teach the silly girl a lesson." Then it said, "ATHENA GOES TO SEE ARACHNE." Then Arachne said, "Oh dear, alas and alack, it is the goddess." I looked at Julie. "Are you kidding? Forsooth? Hark? Alas and alack?"

"What's wrong with that?"

"It's dumb," I said.

"No, it's not," Julie said. "It's cool."

I pointed to the new lines. "I absolutely refuse to forsooth it all over the stage."

Julie giggled and said in a squeaky voice, "Forsooth. Forsooth. Forsooth."

"See? I told you it was dumb," I said. I took the pencil and quickly crossed out all the forsooths and alases and alacks.

Julie looked at what I'd done. "Oh, you old party-pooper," she said.

"Pooper-scooper," I said. "Hey, Julie, did you know that there really is such a thing as a pooper-scooper? It's a little shovel thing for cleaning up dog poop. Honest."

"Starshine."

"Yeah?"

"What does that have to do with Arachne and Athena?"

"Well, Arachne might have had a dog," I said. "And she wouldn't have wanted any poop around. They went barefoot a lot in those days, you know."

Julie looked like she was going to kill me. "Let's get on with the play."

I bowed my head. "Yes, your goddishness."

She chewed on the end of the pencil. "Now what?"

"Athena says, 'Let's have a contest.'"

"That sounds too friendly," Julie said. "She's not inviting her over to play, you know."

I thought for a minute. "How about, 'I challenge you to a weaving contest, silly girl'?"

"Good!" Julie cried. "You're really getting the hang of it, Star."

She wrote down what I'd said. I was proud of myself. We made up some more lines. I kept crossing out the dumb stuff like "hearye" and "pray tell." Arachne was in the middle of hanging herself when Ms. Rooney told us to put everything away and get ready for recess. I looked at Julie. "Poor Arachne," I said, "she'll have to wait till tomorrow to finish the job."

Only she had to wait longer than that. The next day, Wednesday, Ms. Rooney was away. The substitute didn't know anything about the contest and gave us our regular reading lesson. On Thursday Ms. Rooney was back, coughing and sneezing and talking in a gravelly voice.

A horrible thought popped into my head. First Julie had had a cold. Now Ms. Rooney. Some other kids were absent. What if *I* got it — on the day of the contest?

I can't get sick, I said to myself. I absolutely, positively can't. I'll eat lots of oranges. I'll eat grapefruit, even though I hate it. I wonder if tofu burgers are good for colds....

Ms. Rooney blew her nose. "You may start — ah-choo! Excuse me. You may start working on your myths. Remember, the contest is a week from today."

A week! Oh God.

On my way to the back of the room, I passed Lucy Chatham's desk. At the top of her paper she'd written,

PERSEPHONE — THE GODDESS OF SPRINGTIME. Along the side of the paper there were lots of doodlings — but no poetry. She was chewing on the end of her pencil with a very worried look on her face.

Poor kid, I thought. What on earth could she rhyme with Persephone? I tried to think of a word. The closest I could come was "symphony." I'm glad I'm not writing a poem, I said to myself.

I sat down beside Julie. She had printed, "ARACHNE HANGS HERSELF AND DIES."She looked at me with a serious expression. "How are you going to do that?"

"Do what?"

"Hang yourself."

I looked at her, dumbfounded. How *was* I going to hang myself? "I'll tell you one thing," I said. "I'm not going to climb on a chair and put a rope around my neck and have you take the chair away."

"I know that," Julie said.

We sat some more. I got an idea. "I could have a piece of rope — say, in my pocket," I said. "At the hanging part, I could take it out, wrap it around my neck, and fall down."

Julie cocked her head to the side. "Yeah, that'll work. Make choking noises and stick your tongue out and twitch around so people know you're dying."

"I will not," I said. "I'll look like an idiot."

"How else will they know?"

"Well, I think if I put a piece of rope around my neck and then fall on the floor, they'll get the idea."

"It would be better if you made it dramatic," Julie said.

"Look, do you want to be Arachne?" I said.

"Nope."

"Then I'll die my own way," I said.

"Oh, all right," Julie said. "OK, you've died. You're lying on the floor. Now Athena'll say, 'Oh, woe is me, what have I done?'"

"Forget the 'woe is me,'" I said.

"Look, if you can die how you like, I can say 'woe is me.'"

I rolled my eyes.

"Oh, woe is me, what have I done?" Julie repeated. "I did not want Arachne to die, I only wanted to teach her a lesson."

"But you made her kill herself, you big meanie," I said.

"Be quiet, you're dead," Julie said. She tapped her pencil on the edge of her desk. "I know. Athena'll kneel down beside Arachne. Then she'll get up and go — " Julie clapped her hand to her forehead. "Forsooth! I have an

89

idea! Arachne loved to weave so much, I'll change her into a spider.''

"I knew you'd get 'forsooth' back in there somehow," I said.

Julie grinned. "Well? What do you think?"

"It's OK," I said, "but you should really say, 'I'll change her into an arachnid,' so people get the idea that spiders are arachnids and arachnids are named after Arachne."

"But nobody knows what arachnid means," Julie argued.

"Well, you could say, 'I'll change her into an arachnid, which is a group of animals like spiders and scorpions and —' "

"Oh, come on," Julie said. "That's ridiculous."

I didn't say anything. I had to admit it did sound funny.

"I'll change her into a spider," Julie said, writing it down. "Then Athena'll walk over to Arachne — "

"I'm lying on the floor this whole time?"

"Yeah. And she'll say, 'Behold, maiden Arachne, I hereby turn you into a spider.'"

"And that's the end?" I said.

"No. You have to turn into a spider."

I looked at her. "How am I going to do that?"

"I don't know. How *are* you going to do that?"

We both put our chins on our hands and thought. I got an idea. "We could draw a picture of a spider on a big piece of cardboard," I said. "It would be off to the side during the play. At the right time I could reach out with my foot and pull it over and hold it up in front of me."

Julie rolled her eyes. "Bo-o-r-r-ing."

We thought some more. Suddenly Julie exclaimed, "A hat!"

"A hat?"

"Yeah," she said excitedly. "We'll make a kind of crown

with six black legs sticking out — "

"Eight," I interrupted. "All the arachnids — "

"OK, eight legs. You know, the body part on the top and the legs sticking out all around the crown. I'll have it hidden somewhere. At the end I'll pull it out and put it on your head."

"I am not wearing a spider hat," I said.

"But Star — "

"I don't care what you say, I'm not wearing a spider hat."

"It would look neat," she said.

"Forget it."

She looked at me. "Well, how are you going to turn into a spider?"

"I don't know," I said.

Ms. Rooney told us to clean up. Quickly Julie printed, ARACHNE TURNS INTO SPIDER and put a big question mark beside it. "Anyway, after that, I'll say, 'May you weave forever and ever.' The end."

"Hooray," I said, and we put the script away.

Chapter Ten

WHEN I got home, I went out to the back porch to check the eggs. Nothing happening. Then I turned around to see how Goldie was doing. She was sitting there, still and calm. "I wrote a play, Goldie," I told her. She didn't look too impressed. "Well, I didn't exactly do it all myself," I admitted, "but I helped." She waved a leg, as if to say, That's more like it, young lady.

I looked at her. Her body had such a nice curve to it, almost like there was a soft round cushion underneath her, and her abdomen was resting on it, with her legs curving over the sides. How could I change from looking like Arachne to looking like that?

All of a sudden I got an idea. Last Halloween my parents went to a costume party as King Arthur and Queen Guinivere. My mom made herself a cape out of some silky, tannish-brown material. She painted it with a special kind of paint, all different colors, and wore it with a ribbon tied around her neck. When she let the cape hang in the back it just looked like a tan cape with nice colors in it. But when she pulled it around her, there was a whole picture of a castle and a knight in armor and all kinds of stuff. It was really neat.

Couldn't I do something like that, I said to myself. Get a big piece of cloth and paint a picture of a spider on it? I'd ask Mom what kind of paint to use. I'd wear the cloth as a cape, as part of my costume. All through the play it'd hang behind me, kind of in folds, so nobody could see what was on it. At the end, when I was lying there dead,

I'd curl my body into a round hump like Goldie's. I'd secretly untie the ribbon. Then Julie'd pull the cloth over me, and it would cover me, with the body part on the top and the legs hanging down over the sides.

I started pacing across the porch. Would that look like a spider? I asked myself. Maybe — if the cloth was big enough to cover me and the spider picture was good. And it sure would be better than wearing a spider hat.

I wondered if my mom had any of that silky material left. And if she would let me use it. I tingled, thinking how smooth and glisteny it was. I went to the workshop. She was sitting on a stool with a sketch pad on her lap. She drew some big, dark lines on the page and muttered, "There...no...God, that's awful...." She tore out the page, crumpled it up, threw it on the floor, and started drawing again.

I stayed in the doorway. "Mom?"

She didn't answer.

"Mom?" ,

"What?" She didn't look up.

Something told me she wasn't in the mood, but I went ahead anyway. "Remember that cape you made when you were Queen Guinivere?"

She didn't answer.

"Mom, do you remember it?"

"Mmm."

I hoped that meant yes. "Well, I was wondering if you had any of that material left. I need a cape for the play."

She drew some more lines, then crumpled that page, too. "Starshine, I'm trying to design a dryad pot."

Tears came to my eyes. I knew my mom hated to be interrupted when she was working on a pot, but this couldn't wait. I only had a week. "You said you'd help me," I said.

She looked up at me. "I know I did," she said in a softer voice, "and I will. I promise. But I've got to solve this dryad thing first."

I blinked back the tears. "How long will that take?" I said. She didn't hear. She was busy sketching and talking to herself. And I knew that there was no way of knowing how long it would take her to give birth. Sometimes it took a day or two, sometimes weeks. And meanwhile, I wouldn't have a cape. I'd have to wear a spider hat and look like a fool.

I went upstairs, picked up my pillow, and threw it across the room. "I hate that dumb old cape," I said out loud. "I hate the play, I hate the contest, I hate the camping trip, I hate the cookies, I hate Charlotte Feldenstock — "

I burst out laughing. How could I hate Charlotte Feldenstock? I didn't even know her. She wasn't even alive. "Sorry, Mrs. Feldenstock," I said under my breath. "I didn't mean it."

On my way to Julie's desk the next day I heard Miranda talking to Lucy. "Wait till you see me as Aphrodite," she was saying. "She was the most beautiful goddess of all, you know. I'm going to have my hair up, all curled, and I'm going to wear these long dangly earrings of my sister's, and a pink gown and necklaces. And eye shadow. And rouge."

Yuck, I said to myself. Whoever heard of a goddess with eye shadow and rouge? Then I had a horrible thought. What if Miranda won?

"Do you think Miranda could beat us?" I asked Julie.

"No way," Julie said.

"She's going to have a real fancy costume," I pointed out. "Jewelry and makeup and all that."

"Big deal," she said. "A speech couldn't be better than a play. Now, have you been thinking about how you're going to turn into a spider?"

I told her my idea about the cape. She grinned and slapped me on the back. "Star, you're brilliant sometimes, you know that?"

"Only sometimes?" I said.

She ignored the question. "Do you need a special kind of paint?" she said.

"I think so," I said. "I'll ask my mom." I didn't want to tell her about the silky material and get her all excited before I knew if there was any left, or if we could use it.

When I got home from school I went right to the workshop and peeked in. My mom was still crumpling sketches and throwing them on the floor. I decided it wasn't the best time to ask. Maybe tomorrow, I thought. Please, Mom, give birth soon.

The next day was Saturday. I put my allowance into my piggy bank. Now I had $4.50. Only $5.50 to go — by next Friday.

After breakfast I went over to Julie's to work on the play. I was excited about going to her house for a change. Her mom was real nice and so were her grandparents. "Stahshine," they called me. But Julie was right when she said it would be too noisy at her house. One brother was building a bird house, one was practicing the drums, one was acting out a battle with toy soldiers, the TV was on, and some cousins popped in to visit. We couldn't concentrate, so we went back to my house. Julie brought lots of strips of material, all different colors, to use for the weaving. My dad helped us make square looms out of thin pieces of wood. Then we stapled strips of material across the frames. During the play we would weave other strips in and out, in and out, like making a potholder. Julie got to paint her loom with gold paint. I didn't. She said Arachne's loom should be plain, because she was poor. I said that was unfair. Julie said that was tough. I pretended to cry. Julie laughed. I got first pick of the strips of material, to even things out.

Later we went up to my room and read over the script of the play. "It needs more pizazz," Julie said. "It needs a song."

"You mean, like you and me singing a song?"

"That's what people usually do with songs, isn't it?"

I shook my head. "I'm not singing."

"But Star — "

"If you want to sing, you sing," I said. "I'm not singing."

"A song'll clinch it."

"But I don't have a good voice," I said.

"Your voice is fine," Julie argued.

"Ribbet, ribbet," I croaked.

"Oh, come on."

"La-la-la-la-la," I sang like an opera singer.

"Star."

"Julie, I can't sing in front of all those people."

"Why not?"

"'Cause...'cause...I don't know, I just — "

"The play needs it," she said.

"Really?"

"Really. Come on, just one little song."

"We-ell-ll... OK," I said. "One teeny-weeny song."

"Great!" Julie said. "What rhymes with Arachne?"

"Back-nee, lack-nee, pack-nee..." I began. "...gack-nee, mack-nee, tack-nee.... Tack me. Attack me. Don't attack me. How's that?"

She gave me a dirty look and started humming to herself.

The tune sounded familiar. "Hey, that's 'Jeremiah Was a Bullfrog'!" I said.

Julie nodded and kept on humming, then cleared her throat. "How's this? 'Arachne was a fair maiden, Athena was a goddess strong.'"

"Hey, not bad," I said. I hummed those two lines to myself. "Then how about, 'Arachne said, I can weave the best of all '?"

"All right!" Julie said, slapping my leg. "Now, let's see...goddess strong...goddess strong...strong, song, wrong, long...I know — 'Arachne said, I can weave the best of all. Athena said, Not for long.'"

"But she doesn't say 'Not for long' in the play," I said.

"Same idea," Julie said. She wrote down what we had so far:

> *Arachne was a fair maiden*
> *Athena was a goddess strong*
> *Arachne said, I can weave the best of all*
> *Athena said, Not for long.*

We sang it through a few times. "Now for a chorus," Julie said.

I hummed the tune of the chorus to myself. Then I sang, "'Who-o-o will win? Who-o-ose will be the best?' How's that?"

"The who-o-o sounds like an owl," Julie said.

"Well, that's how it is in the real song," I said. "Jooooy to the world."

"That's true," Julie said. "OK. 'Who will win? Whose will be the best?'" She wrote those two lines down. "Arachne and Athena, weave and spin," she sang.

"Athena is a great big pest," I added.

Julie poked me with her elbow.

"Ow!" I said, then moved aside as she tried to jab me

again. "I take it back. Let's see...'One of you will win the test.'"

"Star, you're a genius," Julie said, scribbling down my line. Then we started on the second verse. It was rough. We couldn't think of any rhymes. I was ready to chuck the song, but Julie said no. We went through dozens of lines, and finally figured out a verse. The whole song went:

Arachne was a fair maiden
Athena was a goddess strong
Arachne said, I can weave the best of all
Athena said, Not for long.

Who will win? Whose will be the best?
Arachne and Athena, weave and spin
One of you will win the test.

Arachne started weaving that morning
Athena that afternoon
The goddess did some weaving that was mighty fine
But Arachne aced it on her loom.

Who will win? Whose will be the best?
Arachne and Athena, weave and spin
One of you will win the test.

We sang it all the way through. Then we went downstairs and tried it out on my dad. "Terrific!" he said, smiling. "Aced it on her loom," he said with a chuckle. "I'll bet you guys ace that contest."

Julie and I grinned at each other. Then I got us a snack of bricks and milk. Julie liked bricks now. I'd showed her how to dunk them. When she left, she said, "See you, Arachne."

"See you, Athena," I called. I felt good. The play was coming together. Now all we needed was a spider cape — and a little luck.

Chapter Eleven

MY MOM wasn't at the table the next morning. She'd gone straight to the workshop. I didn't know if that was good news or bad news. It might mean she was close to giving birth. It might not. Whistling "Zippedy Doo-dah," my dad dished out oatmeal for Peggy and me. I'd just taken a mouthful when the phone rang. "It's for you," my dad said, handing me the phone.

"Hi, kiddo," I said, figuring it was Julie.

"I beg your pardon?" a man's voice said.

"Oh — uh, hello?"

"Ms. Shapiro?" the man said.

"Yes."

"Morgan here."

Morgan? Who on earth was Morgan? Oh — Mr. Grandview. "Uh, hi," I said.

"Tell me, my dear, has hatching occurred?"

"Nope. Nothing happening," I said.

"Hmmm," he murmured. "According to my calculations, the spiderlings should have emerged by now. Well, their emergence must be imminent. And the mother — she is doing well?"

I wasn't sure if he meant my mother or the spiderlings' mother. "Goldie, you mean?" I said.

"Goldie, yes."

"Fine," I said.

"Thank goodness for that exhaust pipe," he said.

Suddenly I realized that my mom hadn't fired up the kiln in a while. And she wasn't going to until she had some pots

101

to fire — and she wasn't going to have any until she figured out the dryad thing. Meanwhile, the days were getting colder. How long could Goldie hang on? "Uh... yeah," I said. No sense worrying Mr. Grandview.

"My dear," he said, "I'm very anxious to be informed the moment the spiderlings begin to emerge, or as soon thereafter as possible. Would you phone me as soon as hatching commences — collect, of course?"

"Sure," I said.

"Excellent," he said. He gave me his phone number and I wrote it down. "Much obliged," he added.

"That's OK," I said, and hung up. I had just scooped up a spoonful of oatmeal when the phone rang again.

"It's for you, Ms. Popularity," my dad said with a wink.

"Hello?" I said.

"Hi, kiddo," Julie said.

"*Now* it's you," I said.

"What?"

"Never mind," I said. "What's up?"

"Can I come over?"

"Again?" I said. "I mean — I didn't mean it that way."

"Oh, sure," Julie said, pretending to be insulted. "I know how you really feel about me." She began to sniffle. "Don't try to hide it." Now she was sobbing into the phone. "If you don't want me to come — "

"Enough, enough," I interrupted. "Come over right away."

Julie giggled. "Be there in a minute."

When she came, she was carrying a plastic grocery bag. "What's in there?" I said.

"You'll see," she said with a sly smile.

We went upstairs. Julie put the bag down and took off her jeans and socks. She was wearing a white, long-sleeved leotard. She left that on. Then she reached into the bag, pulled out a pair of sandals, and put them on. "May I ask why you're doing this?" I said.

"You'll see," she said again, giving me that mysterious smile. She took something yellow out of the bag that looked like it must be her mom's nightgown. It had thin, lacy straps and lace around the neck and the bottom. She slipped it on over her leotard. It came down to the floor and covered her feet. "For Athena. What do you think?"

"It's a bit long," I said.

"That's OK, I've got a sash," she said. She pulled a long yellow ribbon from the bag, tied it around her waist, and pulled the nightgown up so it folded over the ribbon, until her feet showed. Then she reached into the bag and got a halo-shaped thing made of shiny gold paper with colored streamers hanging down the back. She put it on her head. "How do I look?"

"Uh... interesting," I said.

"Is that all?" She stood in front of my mirror and swished the nightgown around so it hung more evenly. "Don't I look like a Greek goddess?"

I stood behind Julie and looked at her reflection. A Greek goddess? She looked like a kid wearing her mother's nightgown. But I didn't think I'd better say that. So I said, "Sort of." Which wasn't entirely a lie. She did, a little. The sandals helped.

Julie frowned at me in the mirror. "Don't be so enthusiastic."

"Well, I didn't mean — " I began. "You look OK."

She studied herself in the mirror. I studied her too. The more I looked at her, the more I thought the costume did look OK. The nightgown was soft and flowy, the color was a nice light yellow, and even though the crown looked more like it belonged on a princess than on a goddess, the streamers were pretty against her black hair. "Actually, you look good," I said.

She looked at me in the mirror. "Yeah?"

"Yeah." Then a funny thought struck me. "Just like a Chinese Greek goddess."

Julie giggled and made a small bow. "Athena Wong — at your service," she said grandly. "Now for your costume. You have to look like a peasant girl."

"Can't I just wear my raggedy-est jeans?" I said.

"Star..." she said, rolling her eyes.

"Well, I'm supposed to be poor," I said.

She opened my closet door. "Girls didn't wear pants in those days, remember?"

"Oh, yeah," I said. "You know, I've always felt sorry for girls who lived long ago. Skirts and dresses aren't any good for playing. I bet their legs got cold in the winter, too."

Julie wasn't listening. She took a blue smock dress out of the closet and held it up against me. "Too short," she said. She put it back, then pulled out a long green and white striped skirt. "How about this?"

"Not very Arachne-ish," I said.

Julie looked from me to the skirt and back again. "Yeah, you're right." We searched through the rest of the clothes on the rack but didn't find anything good.

"I guess I'll have to wear my jeans," I said, trying to sound disappointed.

"Hey, what's this?" Julie said, pulling out a bunched-up piece of material from the back corner of the closet.

"Put that back!" I yelled.

Julie looked at me in surprise. "Why?"

"'Cause that's the yuck dress," I said.

The yuck dress is the ugliest dress in the world. My mom found it at a garage sale. It's a patchwork dress made of squares, each with a different pattern. Some are striped, some are checked, some are plaid, some are polka dot, some have zigzag lines, some are flowered, and they're all sewn together like in a patchwork quilt. It's got puffy sleeves and two big pockets, and the bottom hangs down loose like a sack. You could hide three kids the size of Peggy under it.

When my mom brought it home that day, she said, "Look at the darling dress I got you, Star."

I took one look at it, said, "Yuck!" and that's what I've called it ever since. When no one was looking, I rolled it up and stashed it in the corner of my closet. My mom seemed to have forgotten all about it. *I'd* even forgotten about it.

Until now.

"It's perfect," Julie said, holding the dress up to me.

"Forget it," I said.

"This is the dress for Arachne," she said.

"Julie, put it back. I won't wear it."

She pointed at the pockets. "Look, it even has a pocket for the rope."

"I don't care," I said. "It's hideous."

"I know," Julie said.

"So why are you telling me to wear it?"

"'Cause it's right for the part. The patches'll make you look poor."

I shook my head. "No, they won't. They'll make me look like a scarecrow."

Julie ignored that. "It's raggedy looking," she said, smoothing out the wrinkled material. "It's nice and colorful."

"Yuck!" I yelled.

She took my hand and led me over to the mirror. "Star, it's a play. You have to forget you're Starshine Shapiro and imagine you're Arachne. Look at *my* outfit. I wouldn't be caught dead in this. But for Athena, it looks OK. You get what I mean?"

"Yeah. But I'm still not wearing it," I said.

Julie shrugged. "Well, it's up to you. If you can come up with something better, fine." She took off her costume. I didn't say anything. She put her socks and jeans back on, and went home.

I scrunched up the yuck dress and stuffed it under my pillow. Then I opened my closet door and started searching again. I went through every dress, skirt, jumper, and blouse. You'd think with all that stuff I'd have found something for Arachne. But no. Some things were too modern-looking. Some were too short. Some were too sporty. Nothing looked right for a Greek peasant girl of long ago.

I closed my closet door and leaned against it with a sigh. Hey, wait a minute, I said to myself. If Julie can wear a nightgown, why can't I? I pulled open my pajama drawer. There were my yellow and white striped flannel pajamas... my red and white polka dot shortie pajamas... my green nightgown with Donald Duck on the front... my pink Chinese pajamas with the white trim.... And there, on the bottom, was the new nightgown my grandma had given me. I hadn't even worn it yet. It was white with little blue bunnies. Each bunny was holding a purple carrot. I don't know why the carrots were purple. Maybe the dye didn't work right or something.

I shook the nightgown out, went to the mirror and held it against me. It came down to the floor. Sure, I said to myself. This'll be fine for Arachne.

But then I shook my head. Blue bunnies with purple carrots? Ridiculous. Impossible.

"Forget it," I said out loud to my reflection in the mirror. "You're stuck with the yuck dress."

I threw the nightgown back into the drawer, climbed onto my bed, and hugged my knees to my chest. For a while I just sat there. Then I began to think of everything I hated about the play. "Number one," I said out loud, counting on my fingers, "I don't know how to act and I'll probably bungle it up. Number two, it'll look dumb when I kill myself. Number three, I have to sing in front of the whole school. Number four, I have to wear the yuck dress. Number five, if Mom doesn't give birth soon and help me make a cape, I'll have to wear a spider hat."

I stared at my five outstretched fingers. Five things that

can go wrong, I said to myself. Five reasons to quit.

Yeah. Quit. I thought about how good it would feel to just forget the whole thing. I took a deep breath and thought, That's it. I'll quit. No more song. No more yuck dress. No more spider hat. No more worries.

No more camping trip. When I thought of that, it didn't feel so good. And what would I say to Julie? "Julie, forget it, I can't go through with it, I quit"? I pictured her face, the look in her eyes. How could I let her down like that? How could I let myself down? I'd said I would do it. Part of me wanted to get out of it, and part of me wanted to see it through. I felt like I was on that old seesaw again.

I rolled onto my side and looked at Josephine. Her face was in shadow inside the burrow, but her eyes still shone. "What do you think, Josephine?" I said. She didn't answer. But the gleam in her eye said, Stick with it, kid.

Chapter Twelve

THE NEXT day was Monday. Before school I told Julie I'd wear the yuck dress. She smiled and squeezed my hand. It was a good thing she didn't say, "I knew you'd see it my way." I would've strangled her if she did.

That morning, on my way to her desk, I passed Jimmy and Tommy, who were sprawled on the floor, working on their poster of Pandora. In the middle was a picture of a girl with her mouth open. I guessed she was supposed to look surprised or scared, but she really looked like she was showing her tonsils to the doctor. Next to her was a box, with all kinds of monsters coming out of it. They were labelled GREED and HATRED and LAZINESS in wiggly letters. But they didn't look like greed and hatred and laziness, they looked like monsters from comic books. One had long fangs. Another had big, pointy ears and long, spiky fingernails. Coming out of their mouths were bubbles that said stuff like, "Ooooohhh" and "Aaarrggghhh!" Jimmy looked up and saw me. 'What're *you* staring at?" he said.

"Nothing," I said, turning away.

"Hey, man, don't talk to Uh-ratch-nee," Tommy said.

Jimmy chuckled. I walked away, pretending not to hear. "Jimmy and Tommy started that Uh-ratch-nee stuff again," I told Julie.

"Just ignore them," she said.

"I did."

"Good," she said.

We started practicing the play. ''I am Arachne, a peasant

girl,'' I began. "I come from a poor family. But I am a terrific weaver." I sneezed. Ah-choo! "Sorry. 'The best weaver in all of Greece.'" I paused and peeked at the script. "Uh — no one can weave better than me. Not even Athena, the goddess who taught me how to weave." I sneezed again.

Julie put her hands on her hips. "Maiden Arachne is boasting she can weave better than me. How dare she say that!"

Just then Jimmy came by, on his way to the pencil sharpener. "Hi, Uh-ratch-nee," he said.

I didn't look.

"Hey, scratch me, Uh-ratch-nee," he said in a teasing voice.

Julie and I looked at each other. I was dying to turn around and tell him to shut up, but I didn't.

"Hey, is this what's going to happen in your play?" he said.

I couldn't help it. I turned and looked. He was scratching under his arms like a monkey and making a funny face. I thought he meant that he was going to do that during the play, to distract us. "You wouldn't dare!" I yelled.

For a second Jimmy looked confused. Then he grinned. "Thanks for the idea, Uh-ratch-nee!" he said, walking away.

I looked at Julie. I knew something had just gone wrong, but I didn't know what. "What happened?" I said, sneezing.

"I think he meant, were *we* going to do that in the play," Julie said.

"I thought he meant *he* was going to."

"And when you said, 'You wouldn't dare' — " she began.

"I gave him the idea," I finished. I clapped my hand to my forehead. "Oh, Julie, what have I done?"

"Don't worry, he won't really do it," she said in a shaky

voice.

"Yes, he will. I dared him." Ah-choo!

"He can't," Julie said. "He'll get kicked out of the gym."

I shook my head. "You know Jimmy. He'll find a way."

Julie put her hand on my arm. "Well, so what. We'll ignore him. We're not going to let that creep ruin it for us."

"Right," I said. But I was thinking, If he does that during the play, I'll – I'll – I don't know what I'll do.

Julie tapped me on the shoulder. "Come on, let's rehearse."

We started again. Julie knew her part by heart already. I had to peek at my script sometimes. My nose was running like crazy and I kept sneezing. Over and over I had to stop, go to Ms. Rooney's desk, get a tissue, and blow my nose. Each time I got up I lost my place in the script. Julie sighed loudly, as if I was wasting time on purpose. But I couldn't help it, could I?

"You better take your script home today and practice," Julie said when Ms. Rooney told us to clean up.

"I was going to," I said in an annoyed voice.

At recess I didn't feel like playing. Julie and I sat on our bikes and swung our legs. "Have you spoken to your mom about the spider cape?" she asked.

I shook my head. "She hasn't given birth yet."

"Star, the play is only three days away."

"Four, if you count the day of the contest," I said, then sneezed.

"But you can't," Julie argued. "It has to be ready by then."

"I know that," I said.

"So why'd you say there were four days?" she said, irritated.

"I don't know," I said. "Forget it."

"Well, what are you going to do?"

Ah-choo! "I don't know," I said.

"You don't know! That's a great help."

"Well, what am I supposed to do?" I said, wiping my nose. "There's no point asking her until she's given birth. Believe me, I know. It's not my fault she got into dryads. Things were going so great with dragons, too."

"Star, we can't wait any longer," Julie said, facing me. "We've got to do something."

"Like what?" I said.

"Either make a cape ourselves or make a spider hat."

"I am not wearing a spider hat," I said loudly. Ah-choo!

Julie put her hands on her hips. "Well, make a cape then."

"I don't know what kind of paint to use. It was a special kind of paint."

"Look, Star, I'm going to make you a spider hat tonight. If you make a cape, great. You won't have to wear the hat. But at least we'll have something."

I gave a huge sneeze. "I'm getting a cold," I said.

"Oh, great," Julie said. "That's just great."

"Well, you gave it to me," I said. The bell rang. We went inside without saying anything more. I felt worse as the day went on. I got a scratchy feeling at the back of my throat. I kept sneezing, sniffing, swallowing, and blowing. By the end of the day I felt awful. When I got home, I found a note on the kitchen table. It said, MOM'S AT THE LIBRARY. PEGGY AND I ARE SHOPPING. BE HOME AROUND 4:00. HAVE A SNACK. DAD.

I wasn't hungry. I sat at the kitchen table with my head in my hands and thought about how to turn into a spider. I thought and thought until my head felt like a great big muddle. Finally I decided that the only way to get out of wearing a spider hat was to go ahead and make a spider cape myself.

I went to the linen closet and found an old white flannel sheet with a few holes in it. I knew I shouldn't use it without asking. But there was no one to ask, and I had to get going. I tucked the sheet under my arm, hoping it would be OK. Then I went to Peggy's room, got a jar of black poster paint and a paint brush, and went out to the back porch. I spread the sheet on the porch floor. Then I took a good look at Goldie and went to work.

The black paint soaked into the sheet all right. In fact, the sheet seemed to drink up the paint; before I knew it, my brush was dry. To speed things up, I poured a puddle of paint onto the middle of the sheet and began to spread it around to make the spider's abdomen. But I poured a bit too much. I spread the paint and spread it... and spread it and spread it. The abdomen got bigger and bigger. Finally I decided I'd better just let the rest of the puddle soak through, because if I spread it any more, I'd have no room for the legs.

I dipped the brush into the paint and started stroking the first leg. It came out all right. I even managed to show the different segments. While I was doing the second leg, I noticed that the abdomen was growing. By itself. The paint was soaking into a wider and wider circle. It was like a TV commercial for paper towels, when they show you how well their brand absorbs stains. After a while it didn't look like a circle anymore, it looked like a blob. A big lumpy black blob.

My eyes stung with tears. Don't cry, I said to myself, don't don't don't don't. Just finish it. If only it'll stop growing, I can smooth out the edges later.

Somehow I held back the tears. I kept painting legs. At the same time I kept an eye on the blob. It spread a little

113

more, until the puddle had soaked as far as it could. By then the blob took up most of the sheet. It looked like a huge black stain with eight little twigs sticking out of it.

Tears started trickling down my face. I began to sniffle. I sneezed three times. I began to cry. My nose was running and mixing with the tears.

Then I had a horrible thought. I lifted up the sheet and looked underneath. Sure enough, there was a black, blob-sized mark on the wood of the porch floor.

Then I really sobbed. I'd ruined the spider cape, and I'd have to wear a spider hat, and I'd made a mess of the porch, and I'd really catch it for that, and I'd probably catch it for using the sheet without asking, too, and I had a cold, and the whole thing was a big fat rotten disaster.

When I stopped crying, I lifted up the sheet and laid it over the porch railing to dry. Then I got a bucket full of water and splashed it over the black mark. It got watery, spread out some, and began to trickle down through the cracks between the boards. The stain didn't disappear, but it lightened up a bit.

Then I went upstairs, got into bed and slept for a long time. I remember my dad coming into my room and asking if I wanted supper, and going out again. When I woke up my nose was stuffed, my head throbbed, and my throat felt like someone had been scratching it with a tiny rake.

I changed into the bunny and carrot nightgown and went downstairs. Peggy was asleep. From the sound of the potter's wheel I knew my mom was in the workshop. I followed my dad's whistling to the kitchen. He was washing up the supper dishes. When he heard me he turned off the water and faced me. "What happened out back?"

I groaned. I'd forgotten all about it. "I tried to make a spider cape," I said. "For the play."

"Without putting anything underneath?"

"I forgot," I said in a low voice.

"That's quite a stain."

My eyes filled with tears. "It's still there?"

"It certainly is."

Tears started rolling down my cheeks. "Forever?"

"Maybe."

I started blubbering. "I — I'm so-o-rr-ry."

He took me on his lap and stroked my hair. "Everybody makes mistakes. Next time try to think things through a little better, OK?"

Still sobbing, I nodded. I was making an awful mess on his shirt.

"What's this about a cape?" he asked.

I stopped crying, blew my nose, and explained about the cape and about Julie's idea for a hat. "To tell you the truth," he said, "I like Julie's idea."

"Dad!"

"Well, I do," he said. "As far as a cape goes, I'm afraid I can't help you. Mom's the one who knows about fabrics and dyes and all that."

"But she's — " I began.

"I know," he interrupted. "This dryad thing has been a real tough one. But I'll tell you something. I think she's nearly in labour."

"Yeah?" I said, turning to face him.

He nodded. "There was a little sparkle in her eye when she went to the shop tonight. That's usually a good sign."

I sighed. Then I gave a huge sneeze. "God bless you!" my dad said. "Are you hungry? Want some tea and toast?"

"OK," I said.

He made me a cup of almond tea, my favorite, and a slice of toast with butter, honey and cinnamon. It tasted good, but I still felt crummy. There was only one thing that could comfort me: *Charlotte's Web*. I took a copy off my shelf, climbed into bed, and started reading it for the fourth time.

Chapter Thirteen

THAT NIGHT wasn't a very good one. I kept waking up with my nose all stuffed on one side. I'd flip over and wake up later with the other side all stuffed up. By morning, the inside of my head felt like it had thickened into paste. I knew I couldn't go to school. And I realized that I might not get better in time for the contest. But I felt too crummy to get upset about it. I slipped on my bathrobe and went to the workshop. My mom was alone in there, sitting at her work table. Beside her on a shelf were five or six vases in the shape of naked women. I figured they must be dryads. Some were tall and thin. Some were short and fat. None of them looked too great. My mom was working on another. "Hi, Mom," I said.

"Hi, Star." At least she was talking. "Feeling any better?"

"No," I said, and sniffed to prove it.

She didn't answer, just kept molding the clay with her fingers. "Where's Dad and Peggy?" I asked.

"He took her to the park so I could have some peace and quiet."

"Oh," I said. I'd better not talk too much, then.

My mom took a small knife and scraped some clay away from the dryad's legs. I stepped closer. "Hey, Mom, remember that cape I need for the play?"

"Cape?"

"For when Arachne turns into a spider," I reminded her. She didn't answer. "Remember, Mom?"

"Mmm-hmm," she said. I knew that voice. It was the voice she used when she was in another world. When she wasn't really listening. When she was answering to get rid of you.

"I need one real soon," I said.

She leaned closer to the pot and shaped a foot. "Why don't you make one, then?"

"I did," I said. A lump rose in my throat. I swallowed hard. "I made a mess. It didn't turn out."

She turned the dryad around. "Oh, yeah, I remember Dad said something about a black sheet."

A white sheet, I began to say. But it was black now. And what difference did it make, anyway? "So could we make one together?" I said.

Her eyebrows frowned as she examined the head. She didn't answer.

"Could we, Mom?"

"As soon as I make one successful dryad."

"But Mom — " I began. She glanced at me and I saw tears shining in her eyes. She squashed the vase with the palm of her hand, smashing it down until it was a lump of clay. Then she rested her chin on her hands, looking at the floor.

I decided this wasn't the best time to argue. I left the workshop and went out to the porch to see if the spider cape was dry yet. The sheet was still hanging over the railing. The black part looked real stiff, and it didn't look at all like a spider. When I touched it, little flakes of black paint fell off and fluttered to the floor. It was dry, all right. I pulled the sheet partway off the railing. More flakes of paint fluttered off, landing on my bathrobe, my socks and the floor. Where the sheet had been folded over the railing, it had dried in that shape, stiff as cardboard. I tried to flatten it out. Huge flakes of black paint cracked off. I slid the sheet back onto the railing, fitting the bent part right over the railing where it had been before.

I stood there and looked at my black hands with tears in my eyes. The cape was a flop. My mom wouldn't give birth in time. I'd have to wear a spider hat. I imagined the snickers I'd hear, especially from Jimmy and Tommy. A few tears squeezed out. I wiped my eyes, then remembered my black hands. I went to the bathroom. There were black smudges over one eye and on the other cheek. I looked like a pirate. Laughing and crying at once, I washed my face and hands and got back into bed.

When I woke up I felt a teeny bit better. I had some bricks and milk. Then I remembered that I should go over my lines, just in case I got better in time. When I started saying them, it sounded silly for Arachne to be talking to herself, so I read Athena's part, too. But every time I looked at the script to see what Athena was supposed to say, I peeked at my next line. I told myself not to. I knew I was cheating. But I couldn't help it. My eye just slipped down there before I could stop it.

Just as Arachne was saying, "I can still beat you, Athena," my dad and Peggy came in.

"Begin to weave," I said in Athena's voice. "We will soon see if you are really the best weaver in all of Greece."

"Who dere?" Peggy said, looking around to see who I was talking to.

"No one," my dad answered. "Star's just practicing her lines."

"Hey, Dad, would you read Athena's part?"

"Sure," he said, lifting Peggy onto his lap. "Listen, Pumpkin."

I cleared my throat. "I am Arachne, a peasant — "

"You not Aracky," Peggy said. "You Stah."

"Ssshh," my dad said. "It's just pretend. Start again, honey."

"I am Arachne, a peasant girl," I said. "I come from a poor family. But I am — "

"Why Stah say we poor?" Peggy asked, looking at my dad.

"It's just make believe," he said. "Be quiet and don't interrupt, OK?" She nodded as if she'd never interrupt again in her whole life.

"No one can weave better than me," I said. "Not even Athena, the goddess who taught me how to weave."

"Maiden Arachne is boasting she can weave better than me!" my dad said in a dramatic voice. "How dare she — "

Peggy put her finger to her lips. "Ssshhh," she said, frowning at my dad. "Don't int'up."

My dad and I laughed. "It's OK, Pumpkin," he said. "I'm helping Star rehearse."

"I help, too," Peggy said.

The only help you could give would be to get lost, I thought.

"This is just for big people," my dad said.

Peggy stuck her lip out. "I wanna help."

My dad shook his head. "Sorry, Peggy, you can't."

She stuck her lip out farther. Get ready for a tantrum, I thought.

"I tell you what," my dad said. "If you leave Star and me alone while we practice, I'll play Buckin' Bronc with you after." Buckin' Bronc is a game where my dad gets on his hands and knees and Peggy sits on his back and he wiggles and rears up until she falls off. She loves it. She could play it for hours.

Peggy's pout turned into a grin. "OK!" she said, and ran to her room.

I smiled. "Thanks, Dad."

He smiled back, "Quick thinking, eh?"

We started again from the beginning. I did pretty well.

My voice sounded froggy when I sang the song, but I remembered the words.

"I'll tell you, Star," my dad said, handing me the script when we were through, "you and Julie are going to knock their socks off." I grinned, thinking of Ms. Rooney and the other teachers and students walking around the school without socks.

Peggy's door opened. "Ready?" she yelled, running across the living room to my dad.

Laughing, he got onto his hands and knees. "Yes, Peg. And you were very good. Wasn't she, Star?"

That was easy to answer. She was always good when she wasn't around.

Beaming, Peggy climbed onto my dad's back. "Go, Bronky," she yelled, kicking him with her feet.

Just then the phone rang. I answered it. "You sick?" Julie said in a worried voice.

"Yeah," I said.

"How sick?" she said.

I didn't feel like telling her that I felt a smidgen better. "Well, I don't have a fever," I said.

"That's good. You sound awful."

"Thanks a lot," I said.

"Well, you do," Julie said with a giggle. "Are you coming to school tomorrow?"

I cleared my throat loudly. "I don't know."

"Star, you've got to get better. The play's the day after tomorrow. We have to have a dress rehearsal tomorrow after school."

"If I'm better," I said.

"For God's sake, Star, you almost sound like you hope you *don't* get better in time."

"Yes, I do!" I said. "I mean, I *do* hope I get better. What do you think, I want to miss the contest?"

"If you want to know the truth, it's hard to tell."

"Julie!"

"Well," she said. There was a pause. "Anything doing with the cape?"

I told her what had happened.

"It's a good thing I made the hat," she said as if she'd saved our lives. "It came out real good," she added proudly. "I'll bring it to school tomorrow and show you. Hope you feel better."

"Thanks," I said. We hung up. I put my chin in my hands. Julie's right, I admitted to myself. I do hope a teeny bit that I don't get better in time. Well, not really, but — oh, I don't know. "I'm scared," I said out loud. "Nervous, worried, frightened, terrified..." I ran out of words and sneezed.

The next morning I felt crummy, but better. I knew that I was well enough to go to school. I didn't want to go. I didn't want to see the spider hat or have a dress rehearsal. But I did want to go to Dogwood Lake. I wanted to try out my new sleeping bag and hunt for spiders. I wanted to find out if Julie and I really were going to knock their socks off. But —

I lay in bed, watching the minutes flip by on my digital clock. 7:36. 7:37. Choose, I said to myself. Either pretend you're sick and stay in bed for the next four days, or go ahead with it. 7:39. I remembered what my dad had said the day I'd decided to do the play: Nothing ventured, nothing gained. I lay there, thinking about that with a crumpled-up tissue in my hand. It's true, I thought. I wish it wasn't, but it is. If I don't try, I'll never have a chance of making it. I'll never know if I could have done it. 7:42. I took a deep breath and swung my legs over the edge of

the bed.

When I got to school, Julie met me with her lunch box in one hand and a brown grocery bag in the other. We went to the far corner of the playground, away from everybody, and she opened the bag. At first all I saw was a jumble of black shapes. Then I made out the crown part. It was a band of cardboard, painted black. In the front there were two round parts, like on a snowman. The lower ball was round and fat. The top ball, which was a little smaller, had blue eyes, a green nose, and a red grin painted on it. Two long black pipe cleaners sticking out from the top of the head were supposed to be antennae.

Then I saw the legs. Each was made of two toilet paper rolls, joined together so they bent, like a knee. They were painted black, and were attached to the crown part, four on each side.

"Well?" Julie said, beaming.

"Where'd you get all the toilet paper rolls?" I said.

Her smile faded a little. "Around the house," she said.

"Spiders don't have antennae," I said.

Her smile faded all the way. "Star!" she said in a hurt tone. "Is that all you have to say?"

I looked at the hat again. It wasn't bad. In fact, it was good. I just didn't want to wear it. "It's great," I said. "Very realistic. Except for the antennae. And the grin."

Julie beamed again. "Here, try it on." She put it on my head. It fit perfectly. "Pretty good guess, huh?"

I nodded. The toilet-paper-roll-legs went flap-flap against my head. The school bell rang. Very carefully I lifted the hat off my head and put it back in the bag.

"Now our costumes are all set," Julie said cheerfully.

"Right," I said.

Chapter Fourteen

THE SCHOOL was buzzing with excitement about the contest. In the halls, kids were discussing their costumes, their posters, their poems. Teachers were scurrying around with scissors and masking tape. In spite of my cold and everything else, I couldn't help feeling some of the excitement.

And I began to feel a little better. But my voice got hoarser and hoarser. By recess it was pretty froggy. By lunch it was gravelly. By the end of the day it was a loud whisper.

As Julie and I walked to my house she kept asking me how I felt, but as soon as I opened my mouth to answer, she said, "No! Don't talk! Save your voice."

"I'll have lemon juice and honey when I get home," I said.

"What?"

"Lemon juice," I said in a loud whisper.

"Ssshhh! Don't talk," she commanded.

The lemon juice and honey helped a little. We went up to my room and changed into our costumes. I helped Julie fluff up the nightgown around the waist, and she zipped my yuck dress up the back. I put the rope in my pocket, then looked in the mirror. My heart gave a little flutter of dismay. "Yuck," I said.

Julie didn't hear — or at least she pretended not to.

"Let's go," she said.

I walked to the middle of the room. "I am Arachne," I began hoarsely, speaking as loudly as I could.

"Just whisper," she said. "Save your voice."

I began again in a whisper. It wasn't very hard since that's about all the voice I had anyway. Everything went OK until we got to the part where Arachne wins the contest. Athena says, "I can't believe a peasant girl has beaten me at weaving, which is one of my greatest talents." The trouble is, she has a line earlier in the play that goes, "She'll never be able to beat me because weaving is one of my greatest talents." Sometimes I get those lines mixed up and answer with the wrong line.

Julie started her line. "I can't believe a peasant girl...."

Just then the spider hat caught my eye. Oh God, I thought, I absolutely, positively can't put that thing on my —

I felt a poke. Glaring at me, Julie said, "Which is one of my greatest talents."

"Oh — uh... That doesn't matter, I can still beat you, Athena" I said.

"We shall see, foolish maiden — no, wait a minute, that's not right," Julie said.

"Where are we?" I said.

"I said, 'One of my greatest talents,'" she said.

"Right," I said, "and I said, 'That doesn't matter, I can still beat you, Athena.'"

"No, no, no!" Julie yelled. "Not *that* 'one of my greatest talents!'"

"Oh," I said, swallowing. "The *other* 'one of my greatest talents'!"

"Yes," Julie hissed. "Come on, Star, pay attention."

"I'm trying," I said as tears rushed to my eyes. "You don't have to yell."

"I didn't yell," Julie yelled, "I — "

"Yes, you did so yell," I shouted back.

Suddenly we heard a strange sound. It was a mixture of a laugh and a whoop and a shriek and a cheer, and it went through the whole house. I grabbed Julie's arms. "She gave birth!" I yelled. "Wait here, I'll be right back."

I tore downstairs and rushed into the workshop. My mom was standing in the middle of the room with her arms stretched wide. She was laughing and tears were rolling down her cheeks.

"Star!" she cried. "I got it! It's the legs! The legs have to be integrated into the base!" She flung her arms upward. "Oh, Star, I'm so happy!"

We hugged each other. "I've been dreadful," she said. "Oh, honey, I know it's been hard for you and I'm truly sorry. You've been asking for help and I couldn't get my head out of dryads and — " Her voice choked and I felt her body shaking.

I pushed my face against her shoulder and burst out crying. "Mom," I blurted out between sobs, "the play... tomorrow... scared..." For a minute I was crying too hard to speak. Then I said, "And I've lost my voice," and sobbed even harder.

My mom held me. We both wiped our eyes. Then she lifted my face and said, "Is it too late to help you with the play?"

"No! It's not! Oh, Mom — " I nearly started all over again.

She put her hands on my shoulders, then gave me a strange smile. "I was wondering what happened to that dress."

I gulped. "Oh, it just kind of — well, it got buried in my closet for a while."

She shook her finger at me. "You rascal," she said, grinning. "Now, I do have some of that tan material left, and I'm pretty sure there's some dark brown fabric paint. Can the spider be brown?"

I nodded.

"What do you say we whip you up a cape after supper?"

For a minute I just stood there. Then I threw my arms around her neck. "Oh, Mom!" I said hoarsely, and ran upstairs. Julie was waiting in the doorway. I told her what had happened. Then I picked up the spider hat. "Guess I won't be needing this," I said. I was going to drop it into the wastebasket, but something told me that would hurt Julie's feelings, so I put it back in the paper bag.

"Aaawww," Julie said, "it would've looked great."

"Save it for Halloween," I told her. "You can be Spider Lady."

"Great idea!" she said.

"Where were we?"

"You just won the contest," Julie said.

"Oh, right," I said, picking up my loom. I took the rope out of my pocket, wrapped it around my neck, and fell gracefully — at least, as gracefully as I could — onto the floor. Then, while Athena was saying her lines, I curled my body into a ball and pretended to pull a silky, beautiful tan and brown cape over my head.

My mom and I made the cape in the workshop — with newspapers underneath. The fabric paint was a chocolatey-brown color. We painted a round abdomen and eight long, thick legs. Before the paint was dry, she took a wooden popsicle stick and made short strokes down the legs, to make them look hairy. Afterward, we folded down the top edge and made a band. My mom found a pretty brown ribbon to use for a tie. I threaded it through the band, and the cape was done. We spread it out to finish drying.

Before bed I gathered all the things I'd need for the play: the yuck dress, the rope, sandals, my script, the cape, the loom and strips of cloth. They made a pretty big pile. I got a small suitcase from the hall closet and packed everything in it.

When I got into bed I felt scared, happy, embarrassed, and excited all at once. I closed my eyes. "God," I prayed, "let me remember my lines. And don't let me trip. And let me have my voice back." I opened my eyes, then shut them again. "Oh yeah," I added. "Please let me win."

In the morning my voice was still hoarse, but a little better. I couldn't eat breakfast. I nibbled at a piece of toast, took a few bites of granola, then put down my spoon.

"Try and eat, Star," my mom said. "You'll do better if you've got something in your stomach."

I shook my head. "I can't." She patted my hand as if

she understood.

"I'll give you a ride," my dad said.

"Yeah?" I said, surprised. I hardly ever get a ride to school. My mom and dad think fresh air makes your brain work better.

My mom gave me a tight hug. "I'm real proud of you, Star. You've used your creativity and haven't been afraid to take chances. You'll do great, I just know it." She punched me lightly on the arm and said, "Break a leg, kid."

I drew back. "That's not very nice," I said.

My mom and dad laughed. "It's just an expression that theatre people use," my dad said.

"Means good luck," my mom added.

"Oh," I said. "Thanks."

When my dad and I got to school I took his hand. "Dad — I'm scared," I said.

"Of course you are," he said.

I looked at him. I'd expected him to say, Don't be silly, there's nothing to be scared of. Grown-ups are always telling you you're not scared when you know you are. "Everybody's scared when they try something for the first time," he said. "It's perfectly natural."

It was nice to know I was normal, but it didn't make me any less scared. "What if I blow it?"

He smiled. "If you blow it, you blow it, I guess." He put up his hand. "Don't get me wrong. I'm sure you won't. But if you do — well, you'll live." He ruffled my hair. "Just remember to forget you're Starshine."

"Forget I'm Starshine?"

"Mmm-hmm. Pretend you're Arachne. Try to get inside her head and see the world through her eyes. You'll become her. You'll act better. And meanwhile, you'll forget to be afraid."

Anything that could make me forget to be afraid was worth a try. "OK," I said, though it sounded kind of strange.

As I walked to the school yard, Julie ran over. Her eyes had a weird sparkle in them. "I got up real early this morning, Star, it must have been around 5:00! Did you get up early?" Before I could answer, she went on, "I couldn't eat breakfast, could you? Not a bit. My grandma kept telling me, 'Eat! Eat!' But I couldn't. I just bounced around the house until it was time to leave. And here I am!"

I stared at her. I'd never seen her like this. She was like a tape going in fast forward instead of normal speed. Her eyes were shining and her hair was swinging and she went from one sentence to another without even catching her breath.

Suddenly I understood. She was scared. Just plain scared out of her wits — like me.

For a moment I felt better. I wasn't the only one.

But then I thought, Wait a minute. Julie's been in plays before. She's good at it. If *she's* scared, where does that leave me? Petrified, that's where.

My stomach flip-flopped. I was glad I hadn't eaten any breakfast.

The school was like a madhouse. Grade one kids were singing bits of a song about Zeus. Grade two kids were carrying book reports in shiny plastic covers. The grade fives and sixes were rolling their eyes as if they thought it was dumb to get excited about a silly old contest, but I could tell they were excited, too.

All morning our class kept whispering and giggling and fidgeting. Ms. Rooney scolded us once, twice, three times. Finally she snapped a piece of chalk in two and said, "I give up! You people are impossible today." She frowned, but a smile was hiding under the frown. Then she said, "If you have to change into a costume for the contest, do so in the washroom right after lunch. When the bell rings, come back here. We'll go to the gym at 1:00 sharp."

Julie and I got our lunch boxes. I forced myself to eat half a sandwich. Julie didn't eat at all. She tapped her foot against the metal bar at the bottom of her desk. Tap-tap-tap. "Hey, Star," she said, "did I ever tell you about the play our class did last year for the spring concert?" Tap-tap-tap. "It was called, 'Monkey See, Monkey Do.' I was the leader of the monkeys."

"Stop tapping," I said.

"Oh, was I tapping? Sorry." She started drumming her fingers on the desk top. "We had these cloth tails in the back," she went on breathlessly. "In the middle of the play mine came off. Right in my hand! I thought I'd die. But of course I didn't, 'cause I'm still here."

"Oh," I said. I wished she'd quit chattering. It made me more nervous than ever.

Julie glanced at the clock. "12:20!" she said with a gasp. "We've got to get changed. Come on!"

We hurried to the girls' washroom. It was jammed with kids changing their clothes, brushing their hair, putting on makeup. Everywhere you stepped there were piles of clothes, shoes, crowns, costumes. Some grade six girls were standing in front of the mirror, putting on lipstick.

Julie went into a stall and began to change. I stood there with my suitcase in my hand, waiting until the crowd in the washroom had thinned out a bit. I didn't want to be seen in the yuck dress until it was absolutely necessary.

A few minutes later, Julie came out in her costume. When she saw me she pushed me toward a stall. "Get dressed!" she said. "We've still got to put on our makeup!"

I turned and looked at her. "Makeup?"

She grinned. "I snitched some from my mom."

I went into the stall, took off my clothes, and put on the yuck dress and my sandals. I tied the cape ribbon around my neck and looked over my shoulder to make sure the spider picture wasn't showing.

"That's more like it," Julie said when I came out. But I hardly noticed, because there in the middle of the washroom was Miranda. Dressed as Aphrodite. She had on a ruffly pink blouse and a long pink skirt. Around her neck was one of those feathery scarves, bright yellow. She had on three necklaces, all different colors, and dozens of bracelets. She was wearing shiny silver high heels that were way too big for her. She had on lipstick, rouge, and gobs of eye makeup. Her hair was piled high on her head, and there were glittery things in it. She didn't look like Aphrodite. She looked like Miranda trying to look like an eighteen-year-old.

I thought she looked dumb. But a lot of girls in the washroom, especially the younger ones, were staring at her as if she was the most gorgeous thing they'd ever seen. "Oooohh," one little girl crooned, "isn't she bee-you-tee-ful?"

I looked at Miranda and she looked at me. Then she lifted her chin a little higher in the air and flounced out of the washroom, her high heels clomp-clomping on the tile floor.

Julie grabbed my arm and pulled me to the mirror. "Don't worry about her." She handed me a tube of lipstick. "Here, put some on."

I looked at her. She already had a red mouth and was patting rouge onto her cheeks. "Don't you just love putting makeup on?" she said. "I do. It makes me feel so grown up. All the really famous actresses and actors have people who do their makeup for them, did you know that, Star? Wouldn't that be neat, just to sit back and let somebody do your face? But then you wouldn't have the fun of doing it yourself. Ooops, too much eye shadow.''

I thought I was going to strangle her if she said another word. Just to get out of the washroom fast, I quickly painted a smear of red on my lips, dabbed rouge on my cheeks, and brushed a line of blue on each eyelid. Then I stood back and looked at myself. My lips were big and red, and the dress was a wild splash of color below.

Most of the other kids were in the classroom when we got there. When Jimmy Tyler saw us, he started jumping around and scratching under his arms, like he had the other day. ''Scratch me, Uh-ratch-nee,'' he sang, and Tommy joined in.

Julie squeezed my hand. I squeezed hers back. Ignore it, she mouthed to me. I nodded. But if they do it during the play, I thought, I'll die. I'll absolutely die.

Just as Ms. Rooney came in, the principal's voice crackled on the loudspeaker. ''All classes may now proceed to the gym,'' she said. A ripple of excitement went through the class. I clutched my loom and strips of material, felt for the rope in my pocket, and made sure my cape was tied tightly. Our class filed into the hall and joined the other classes marching to the gym.

Chapter Fifteen

A T ONE end of the gym there was a huge banner that said THE MYTHS COME ALIVE. Posters, collages and murals lined the walls. Along one wall there were tables set up, with clay models on them. Behind where we were sitting was another table for the three judges. One of them was Ms. Sanford, our school librarian. The second one was the librarian at our local public library. The third judge was a man I didn't know.

The gym was full of kids, kindergarteners at the front and older kids at the back. Some were in costumes, some in regular clothes. One little boy was holding a small bow and a rubber-tipped arrow. I figured he was supposed to be Cupid. Another kid, a big one, was dressed as a monster. His (or her — I couldn't tell if it was a boy or a girl) face was covered with black makeup, and his (or her) hair stuck out in every direction. I wondered how he (or she) had made it do that.

Ms. Sanford stepped to the front. "Good afternoon, boys and girls," she said, "and welcome to the First Annual Charlotte Feldenstock Memorial The Myths Come Alive Contest. Before we begin, I'd like to introduce the other judges. Susan Milgrove, from the Riley Park branch of Vancouver Public Library." The woman at the back table stood up, smiled at the audience, and sat down. "And Roger Cormorant," Ms. Sanford said, "who teaches ancient Greek philosophy and mythology at the University of British Columbia." The man half-stood in his seat, bowed his head, and sat down. He looked very serious. Not the kind of guy who'd think "Arachne aced it on her loom" was real funny.

Ms. Sanford cleared her throat. "The other judges and I have already looked at the kindergarten class's mural, the book reports by the grade twos, and the models and posters by the grade fives. So this afternoon we will have presentations by grades one, three, four and six. We will announce the winners all together at the end. And just in case you've forgotten, the prize, to be awarded at each grade level, is five dollars and a copy of *Bullfinch's Mythology*." There was a burst of laughter. As if we could have forgotten that! "And now, without further ado, let the myths come alive," Ms. Sanford said. "Grade one class, please."

If there ever was a time when I was glad not to be in grade one, this was it. The kids stood in a bunch. Some of them waved to their big brothers and sisters in the audience. Then they started singing a song to the tune of "Frere Jacques":

> *Zeus and Hera, Zeus and Hera*
> *King and queen, king and queen*
> *Lived on Mount Olympus, lived on Mount Olympus*
> *High and green, high and green.*

After singing it once through all together, they started singing it as a round. By the second line, they'd gotten all mixed up, and the ones who were supposed to finish first slowed down and finished with the others. But the audience gave them a big hand anyway. Grinning and waving, they sat down.

Then it was the third graders' turn. They came to the front and recited a poem called "Up On Mount Olympus High," which they had made up.

Up on Mount Olympus high
Zeus sat on his throne in the sky.
Gods and goddesses, twelve in all
Sat with him in the palace hall
Dining on ambrosia sweet,
Nectar, wine, and other treats.
Next to Zeus was a bucket of thunder
To use if anyone made a blunder.
And when they quarreled, what a fight —
Zeus would make it storm all night!
Oh, up on Mount Olympus high
Zeus sat on his throne in the sky.

As they chanted I turned around and peeked at the judges. Ms. Sanford and Ms. Milgrove were whispering together. Mr. Cormorant was sitting like a statue with his arms folded across his chest. A shiver crept down my neck. I turned back around and thought, Slow down, you guys, take your time. What's my first line? 'I am Arachne, a poor girl. I come from a peasant family.' No, that's not it. 'I am Arachne, a peasant girl. I come from a poor family.' I was clutching the loom so hard my knuckles were white, and the strips of cloth in my other hand were getting damp from sweat. Both verses of the song begin with Arachne, I said to myself. Start weaving with the light green strip. Where's the rope? I lost the rope. Oh, no I didn't, it's here in my pocket.

Julie turned and looked at me. Her eyes still had that glittery, nervous look. I could tell she was really excited. Like, she was scared but she couldn't wait to get going. Not me. I hoped the grade threes' poem went on forever.

The next thing I knew everyone around me was clapping and Ms. Rooney was walking to the front. My stomach tightened into a knot. "Our class studied a variety of myths," she said. "The children have presented them in different ways. Jimmy and Tommy, would you like to tell us about your poster?"

Jimmy and Tommy got up and swaggered across the gym like the coolest dudes in the west. But when they turned around I saw that Jimmy's face was bright red and Tommy looked as though he'd seen a ghost. Stagefright, I thought. Hah. I knew that was mean, but I didn't care. They'd been pretty rotten to Julie and me.

"We did Pandora," Tommy said in a choked voice, pointing to the girl. Say aahhh, I thought. He poked Jimmy.

"Oh – uh, she had this box," Jimmy stammered, his face turning even redder, "and all kinds of bad things came out of it."

"'Cause she" – gulp – "was too curious," Tommy explained.

Jimmy crossed his arms, then put his hands in his pockets. "Hatred," he said. "Greed. Laziness." His voice got softer and softer. "Envy. Dishonesty." His voice faded completely. Tommy grabbed his arm and they walked back to their places. You didn't win, I thought. So there.

"Lucy has written a poem about Persephone," Ms. Rooney said. "Lucy?"

Blushing, Lucy walked to the front. Good luck, I thought. I didn't want her to win, but I felt sorry for her, knowing how much trouble she'd had with the poem.

She cleared her throat. "Persephone," she said. Her voice was so quiet you had to lean forward to hear it.

> *There once was a girl named Persephone*
> *Who was as happy and gay as a pony.*
> *One day when she was dancing around*

Hades caught her and took her underground.
He gave her diamonds and gold
But she didn't want them she wanted to go home,
And up above, the world grew cold.
Then Zeus told Hades to let Persephone go
So plants and trees could grow.
So Hades did, but only for a time.
He said to Zeus, "The rest of the year she's mine."
When Persephone comes up we have spring,
Flowers bloom and birdies sing,
But when she goes down through a crack like a splinter,
The world gets cold, and then we have winter.

I clapped hard for her, and so did the audience. She looked really relieved. I was jealous of her for being finished.

"Miranda?" Ms. Rooney said.

Miranda got up with a swish and a rustle and clomp-clomped to the front. There were ooohs and aaahs from the audience. She folded her hands like an opera singer. "Aphrodite was the goddess of love," she recited. "She was the most beautiful goddess of all." She swept one hand downward, as if to say, Just like me. Ugh, I thought.

"Aphrodite had no mother or father," Miranda went on. "She just rose out of the sea." Miranda wiggled her hands like waves in the sea, then raised her arms like the sun rising. "She rode in a gold chariot pulled by white doves. They pulled her straight to Olympus. When the gods saw her" — Miranda put both hands over her heart — "they thought she was so-o-o beautiful, they made her a goddess and put her on a golden throne. All the gods fell in love with her 'cause she was so lovely. The end." Miranda curtsied right down to the floor, then stood up, smiled at the audience, and started back to her place.

The audience clapped loudly. Some kids began to cheer, and others joined in. The cheering got louder. I turned around and peeked at the judges. All three were clapping hard. Oh, no, I thought. She can't win. She can't —

"Starshine and Julie," Ms. Rooney said.

I froze. Julie grabbed my arm and pulled me to my feet. Oh God, I thought, walking to the front. I am Athena. No, I'm not. I am Arachne. Both verses...the cape...I am a spider. The rope....

Julie put me where I was supposed to stand. I glanced at the audience. There were so many people out there, all I could see was a mish-mash of faces. Then I made out the three judges at the back. Ms. Sanford and Ms. Milgrove were leaning forward, elbows on the table. Mr. Cormorant was leaning back against his chair, arms folded. They weren't smiling and they weren't frowning. It was as if they were saying, OK, let's see.

A sudden movement caught my eve. It was Jimmy and Tommy. Both of them were scratching under their arms and making funny faces. I looked away. A lump rose in my throat. My mouth felt as dry as wood.

"The Story of Arachne," Julie said in a loud, clear voice. Then she moved to the side and nodded to me to begin. I opened my mouth. "I am Arachne," I said. My voice was barely louder than a whisper. I cleared my throat. I was clutching my loom so tightly, it dug into my side. "I am Arachne, a peasant girl," I said, a little louder. My voice sounded so small in the big gym. I swallowed. "I come from a poor family," I said. My voice trembled. I knew I had to calm down, to make my voice sound normal, to swallow down the lump in my throat. But all I could think was, I'm blowing it. I was right. I can't act. I knew it, I knew it, I knew it.

Out of the corner of my eye I saw Jimmy and Tommy doing their monkey thing. I gripped my loom harder. All of a sudden I got mad. You dumb creeps, I thought. I'm not going to let you ruin my play! I'll show you!

I stood up a little straighter. At the same time I looked at Ms. Rooney. She winked at me. I took a deep breath. "But I am a terrific weaver," I said, louder. *There* was my own voice! "The best weaver in all of Greece." I brushed my hand across the loom, as if showing how good a weaver I was. That wasn't in the script. I just made it up on the spot.

I took a step. "I can even weave better than Athena, the goddess who taught me how to weave," I said. I looked at the audience. All I saw were blurry faces. But I felt their eyes. Jimmy and Tommy were still at it, I knew. I ignored them.

Julie walked over. The yellow nightgown swished and the colored streamers fluttered as she moved. She stood up real straight, just like a goddess. "Maiden Arachne is boasting she can weave better than me," she said loudly. "How dare she say that!"

The way Julie spoke gave me the chills. Like, she really was Athena. Suddenly I remembered what my dad said: "Forget you're Star. Pretend you're really Arachne. You'll *become* Arachne, and you'll act better, too." I lifted my chin as I stroked my loom. I might just be a peasant girl, but I could still weave better than Athena. So there.

Julie went on speaking, challenging me to a contest. I stood proudly, moving my hand across my loom. "Yes, Athena, I will have a weaving contest with you," I said. My voice was hoarse, but strong. I glanced quickly across the audience. Jimmy and Tommy were sitting still, watching.

"Begin to weave," Julie said. "We will soon see if you are really the best weaver in all of Greece." We looked at each other. She nodded her head three times, and we started singing. Somehow I remembered to weave the strips and sing at the same time. The melody just came out and I didn't forget any words. When we sang, "Arachne aced it on her loom," I heard some laughter. I glanced up. Mr. Cormorant was smiling!

Before I knew it, it was time for me to kill myself. My fingers fumbled as I pulled the rope out of my pocket, but finally I got it around my neck. As I began to fall, I remembered what Julie had said about making the hanging dramatic. Forget it, I thought, but then I said to myself. Why not? I flung out my arms and fell in a big swoon. Some of the little kids gasped. One kid whispered, "She's dead!" Poor Arachne, I thought.

As Julie spoke her last lines, I slowly curled myself into a ball. At the same time I untied the ribbon of the cape. We hadn't rehearsed this. I hoped it would work. Julie walked over to me. "May you weave forever and ever," she said grandly. Then I felt her pull the cape up over my head and smooth it out across my back. I stayed absolutely still. The gym was quiet.

Then I stood up. Julie and I took hands and bowed. The audience started clapping. They clapped louder. We bowed again. They kept clapping. Even Jimmy and Tommy were clapping. There were some cheers and whistles. I squeezed Julie's hand, and she squeezed me back.

I did it! I said to myself. I actually, really and truly did it! I couldn't believe it, and yet I did believe it. I felt wonderful.

Julie gave me a tug and started pulling me back to our

places. I didn't want to leave. I wanted to stand up there and listen to them clap.

Finally we sat down. "You were great!" Julie whispered. I just grinned back. I was too excited to talk. I didn't see or hear the other kids make their presentations. All I could think was, I did it. I *can* act. And I thought about how my dad was right. Julie had become Athena. And I had become Arachne — a little. And when I did, it felt magical.

The grade sixes presented their myths. Don't ask me what they did; I couldn't tell you. I couldn't concentrate. I wanted to hold on to that wonderful feeling of pretending to be someone else, and having people believe it. I didn't even know if we had done a good job. I figured we must have made some mistakes. I didn't know if we would win. All I knew was that I had acted in a play — and that it had really and truly been fun.

Chapter Sixteen

A FTER THE last grade sixer — which turned out to be
the kid with the black face and wild hair, who was
supposed to be the Minotaur — Ms. Sanford came to the
front. "What marvelous presentations," she said. "I'm
sure Charlotte Feldenstock would be very proud. Now,
the other two judges and I will need about ten minutes to
choose the winners. In the meantime, Ms. Tattler has
graciously offered to lead you in some singing."

My stomach churned. Miranda won, I thought. I'm sure
of it. No, we were better. No, she won. No, we did.

Ms. Sanford, Ms. Milgrove and Mr. Cormorant left the
gym. Ms. Tattler, the grade five teacher, came forward
with her guitar. She started strumming and singing, "I'm
in the mood for singing. Hey, how about you? I'm in the
mood for singing. Hey, how about you?" Everybody joined
in, especially on the clapping and stomping parts. I didn't.
I wasn't in the mood.

The three judges came back in. Ms. Milgrove was carrying
a heavy box, which she put down with a thud. Ms. Sanford
had a handful of white envelopes. The gym got very quiet.
Please, I thought. Please.

"We have had a most difficult job because your presentations were so good," Ms. Sanford said, smiling. "Remember, even if you don't win the prize, you can still be
proud of your efforts." She took three books out of the
box. "For the kindergarten and grade one and grade three,
we have decided to present the prize to the entire class. You
will just have to have a class party to spend the money."

Everyone laughed, and the three teachers came up and took a book and an envelope from Ms. Sanford. Then Ms. Milgrove stepped forward. "For the grade twos, the winner, for her excellent book report on Agamemnon, is Allison Topworth." There was a squeal, and a little girl with long blond braids came to the front.

Then Mr. Cormorant stepped forward. I closed my eyes. "It is with great pleasure that I award the prize for grade four to — " Miranda Stockton, I finished in my mind. Mr. Cormorant stopped. I opened my eyes. He was fumbling with a piece of paper. Finally he got it out of his pocket, then turned it right side up. " — to Starshine Shapiro and Julie Wong."

I jumped up. So did Julie. She squeezed my arm. I hugged her. I hardly breathed as we walked between the seated kids to the front. We won! We really won oh God I can't believe it we won I made it we won!

Mr. Cormorant shook both our hands, then handed me the book and Julie the envelope. He leaned forward and winked. "Don't tell anybody, but Arachne happens to be one of my favorites."

Julie and I went back to our places. I held out the book to her, while putting out my other hand for the envelope. "Swap," I said.

"I changed my mind," she teased. "You can have the book. I'll keep the money."

"Julie!"

Laughing, she gave me the envelope. I laughed, too, from way down deep inside. It felt so good. I made it, I said to myself. All but fifty cents. And I'll get that somehow, I'm sure of it.

I completely missed who won in grade five. For the grade sixes, the winner was the Minotaur. I agreed with the choice. Anyone who was brave enough to go around looking like that deserved to win.

When the last prize had been given out, Ms. Sanford told the teachers to take their classes back to their rooms. Julie and I linked arms and walked together. I felt like I was stepping on clouds of air. As we walked down the hall, Jimmy and Tommy brushed past us. "Good show," Jimmy said in a low voice, trying not to move his lips. "Yeah, Arachne," Tommy added, looking straight ahead.

I winked at Julie. "Thanks," I said. Then I heard a clomp-clomp-clomp. Miranda. She hurried to catch up with us. "Great play, you two," she said. Julie and I squeezed elbows, as if to say, Can you believe this? We thanked her. Then Miranda touched my arm. "Uh... Starshine?" Just then Ms. Rooney came along and asked Julie if she could see *Bullfinch's Mythology*. Julie slipped her arm

out of mine and walked on ahead. Miranda and I were alone in the hall.

"Yeah?" I said.

Miranda looked at me, then looked down. "Uh... the next time you do a play, could I — uh... could I be in it?"

For a minute I thought I'd heard wrong. Then I figured she was teasing. I looked at her face. No, she wasn't. She meant it! "In a play? With me?"

She nodded. "You guys were great. What a story! Look — " She held out her arm. "I've still got goose bumps."

I smiled. "I know what you mean."

"I loved the song," she added. "It looked like fun."

"Uh... yeah, it was fun," I said, amazed at myself.

"So could I?"

"Sure," I said. Why not?

She grinned. "Gee, thanks!" We walked into the classroom together.

The class gave Julie and me a hip-hip-hooray. When Ms. Rooney dismissed us, Julie and I were too excited to change back into our regular clothes. We raced home as fast as we could, stopping first at her house to tell her family the good news, then hurrying to mine.

I dropped the suitcase on top of Peggy's shoe pile. Waving the envelope in the air, I shouted, "We won! We won! We won!" My mom and dad came running from the workshop, my mom splattered with clay and my dad's goggles on top of his head. They hugged me and spun me around, and then hugged Julie, too. Peggy ran into the living room with a paintbrush in her hand and a spot of purple paint on her nose. "Stah won!" she yelled, not even knowing what that meant.

Julie and I told them about the contest and all the presentations and the judges and everything. "Gee, I'd have given anything to see you two perform," my dad said.

"Me, too," my mom said. "Hey, why don't you do it for us right now?"

"Great idea," my dad said. "How about it?"

I looked at Julie. She shrugged, then grinned. "Why not?"

"OK," I said. We got our looms and strips of material and the rope and the cape.

"Why don't we go out on the back porch?" my mom suggested. "You'll have more room." So we did. My mom, dad, and Peggy sat on the swing-chair. Julie stepped forward and announced, "The Story of Arachne," just like at school.

"I am Arachne, a peasant girl," I began. "I come from a poor family. But I am a terrific weaver...." I looked at my mom and dad. The look in their eyes told me they loved me and were proud of me. I felt great. I kept talking. "...the goddess who taught me how to weave."

"Maiden Arachne is boasting she can weave better than me," Julie said. "How dare she say that!"

We said our lines without even thinking. They just came. After a while Peggy slid off the swing-chair and started wandering around the porch. I figured the play must be a little hard for her to understand.

"Yes, Athena, I will have a weaving contest with you," I said.

"What dis?" Peggy said from over in Goldie's corner.

"Don't interrupt, Peggy," my dad said.

"Yeah," I said, annoyed. "Where was I?" I glanced at Peggy again. Then I noticed that she was looking at the hanging plant.

I dashed over to the corner and turned the leaves over. Some of the egg sacs were already empty; you could see the little hollow cocoons. Behind the plant, on the wall,

hundreds of tiny spiderlings were running around, beginning to spin their web. It wasn't a web, really, just a tangle of silk. I knew the babies would live together in it for a few weeks, and then go off to spin their own webs. While I watched, other sacs opened and dozens more spiderlings crawled out and joined in spinning the web.

"They're — they're — oh, look!" I said. It was so beautiful, I couldn't even talk. Julie ran over, then my mom and dad. They stood behind me and watched. More and more babies hatched and joined their brothers and sisters. Soon the spiderlings had made a ragged, yellowish web. Hundreds of them were crawling around in it. I squeezed out from in front of everybody and knelt down beside Goldie. "Hey, Goldie," I said softly, "you're a mom."

All of a sudden I straightened up. "Oh no!" I shouted. "I forgot — I've got to — What time is it? Mr. Grandview'll kill me. Somebody tell me what day it is, quick!" I dashed over to the place where I'd thumb-tacked the paper to the wall and picked up the pencil. Somehow I managed to write down that it was October 26th, the hatching had started at 3:47 P.M., and the weather was sunny. Then I went inside and called Mr. Grandview. When I told him the news, he whooped so loud it hurt my ear. "Tell me, Starshine," he said, "how many spiderlings are there?"

"Oh, gee," I said, "I don't know. Maybe three or four hundred."

"Splendid," he said. "And have they spun their communal web?"

"Yup. They're in it now."

He sighed. "Oh, how I long to see them. What a rare opportunity to study *Nephilia* spiderlings." He paused. Then he said, "Say, I wonder — would it be too much of an imposition if I visited you again? Tomorrow?"

"Sure," I said.

"It *would* be too much of an imposition?" he said sadly.

"Oh, no — I mean, sure, it would be fine."

He gave a great happy sigh. "Thank you, Starshine. I greatly appreciate your kind forbearance."

"You do?" I said, not sure what he meant.

"Yes, indeed," he said. "Oh — one more thing. Those health food cookies you served me last time. Are there any left?"

"Six dozen in the freezer," I said.

"Oh, splendid," he said. "I'm so glad you haven't eaten them all. Would you be so kind as to sell me another box? My wife and I just adore them."

"No trouble," I said.

"Marvelous. See you tomorrow."

I took a box of health food cookies out of the freezer and set it on the kitchen counter. There was another $1.25. That would give me $9.50 plus $1.25; $10.75 altogether. I'd made it with 75 cents to spare! I took a deep breath, went out to the porch, and had a weaving contest with Athena.

The camping trip was terrific. On the way to Dogwood Lake we sang songs and counted Volkswagen beetles and played Geography. Lucy asked if Julie and I would teach the class the song from our play. We looked at each other, grinned, and said, "Sure!" Pretty soon everyone was roaring it out at the top of their lungs — even Jimmy and Tommy.

In the morning, Julie and I explored a patch of woods behind the cabins. We found a dwarf spider and a couple of hammock spiders and a tiny grey one that I didn't know. I'll have to look it up in my field guide.

I gave Julie one of the hammock spiders to hold. She looked at it with a kind of half-fascinated, half-terrified look on her face. But then it started crawling up her sleeve. She shrieked and shook it off. "You're hopeless, kid," I told her.

"Hopeless!" she said, putting her hands on her hips. "You just call me that again and — and — I'll clobber you with *Bullfinch's Mythology!*"

Sometimes when I get into bed and say goodnight to Josephine and Herman, I think of Arachne, and that reminds me of the play, and that reminds me of how good it felt to stand up there and pretend to be someone else and have everybody watch me and clap for me and all.

So I think I'll be a combination arachnologist-actress when I grow up. And I won't even have to change my name. Starshine Bliss would make a terrific stage name, don't you think?

The Story of Arachne

By Starshine Bliss Shapiro and Julie Wong

CHARACTERS: Arachne
Athena

PROPS: — a square loom for each character, with strips of material stapled crosswise to it, and other strips of material for weaving; Arachne should have more colourful strips so her weaving will look nicer
— a piece of rope, about 50 cm long
— a cape with a spider painted on it
— old-fashioned costumes with sandals.

ARACHNE IS ON STAGE

ARACHNE: I am Arachne, a peasant girl. I come from a poor family. But I am a terrific weaver. The best weaver in all of Greece.

ATHENA WALKS ON STAGE

ARACHNE: No one can weave better than me. Not even Athena, the goddess who taught me how to weave.

ATHENA: Maiden Arachne is boasting she can weave better than me. How dare she say that? She forgets I am a goddess. I will have to teach the silly girl a lesson.

ATHENA GOES TO SEE ARACHNE

ARACHNE: (TO THE AUDIENCE) Oh, dear, it is the goddess. (TO ATHENA) Hello, Athena.

ATHENA: I challenge you to a weaving contest, silly girl. We will both weave on our looms. Do you accept?

ARACHNE: Yes, Athena, I do.

ATHENA: (TO THE AUDIENCE) She'll never beat me because weaving is one of my greatest talents.

ARACHNE: That doesn't matter, I can still beat you, Athena.

ATHENA: Begin to weave. We will soon see if you are really the best weaver in all of Greece.

ARACHNE AND ATHENA WEAVE STRIPS OF MATERIAL INTO THEIR LOOMS WHILE THEY SING

Arachne was a fair maiden
Athena was a goddess strong
Arachne said, I can weave the best of all
Athena said, Not for long.

Who will win? Whose will be the best?
Arachne and Athena, weave and spin
One of you will win the test.

Arachne started weaving that morning
Athena that afternoon
The goddess did some weaving that was mighty fine
But Arachne aced it on her loom.

Who will win? Whose will be the best?
Arachne and Athena, weave and spin
One of you will win the test.

ATHENA: There. Let us compare our weaving.

ARACHNE AND ATHENA HOLD OUT THEIR LOOMS

ATHENA: By Zeus, what is this? I can't believe a peasant girl has beaten me at weaving, which is one of my greatest talents.

ARACHNE: I told you I was the best weaver in all of Greece.

ATHENA: It is impossible! I won't stand for it!

ATHENA GRABS ARACHNE'S LOOM, PULLS OUT SOME OF THE STRIPS, THEN PRETENDS TO HIT ARACHNE WITH HER LOOM

ARACHNE: Oh! Oh! I am so embarrassed! I cannot bear to live!

ARACHNE WRAPS ROPE AROUND HER NECK, PRETENDS TO PULL IT TIGHT AND FALLS TO THE FLOOR. ATHENA KNEELS BESIDE ARACHNE

ATHENA: Oh, woe is me, what have I done? I did not want Arachne to die, I only wanted to teach her a lesson.

ATHENA STANDS UP AND CLAPS HER HAND TO HER FOREHEAD

ATHENA: Forsooth! I have an idea! Arachne loved to weave so much, I'll change her into a spider.

ATHENA POINTS TO ARACHNE

ATHENA: Behold, Maiden Arachne, I hereby turn you into a spider.

ARACHNE UNTIES CAPE. ATHENA PULLS CAPE OVER ARACHNE

ATHENA: May you weave forever and ever.

THE END

STARSHINE!